BASED ON A TRUE STORY

A Broken MIRROR

Sara W. Berry

Tupelo, Mississippi

Copyright © 2015 by Sara W. Berry

All rights reserved. This book is protected under the copyright laws of the United States of America, and may not be reproduced in any format without written permission from the publisher.

ISBN: 978-0-9970239-0-9
Printed in the United States of America

Cover Design:
Tracy Applewhite Broome
www.tracybroome.com

Cover photography:
The Art of Life Photography by Joy Ballard
artoflifephotography@aol.com

Editorial Assistance:
Sue Geier, Nashville, TN

Author photography for Sara Berry:
Stephanie Rhea
www.stephanierhea.net

Photography and logo for Kelly Williams:
Tarver Reeder
tarverreeder.prosite.com

Unless otherwise noted, all scripture references are taken from the Holy Bible, New International Version. Copyright 1973, 1978, 1984 International Bible Society. Used by permission. All rights reserved.

Where noted, scripture references taken from New American Standard Bible. Scripture taken from the NEW AMERICAN STANDARD BIBLE®, Copyright © 1960,1962,1963,1968,19 71,1972,1973,1975,1977,1995 by The Lockman Foundation. Used by permission.

Also where noted, scripture references taken from the New Living Translation. Scripture quotations are taken from the Holy Bible, New Living Translation, copyright 1996, 2004. Used by permission of Tyndale House Publishers, Inc., Wheaton, Illinois 60189. All rights reserved.

Also where noted, scripture references taken from the New Life Version. Copyright © 1969 by Christian Literature International. Used with permission.

Published by Bethel Road Publications, Tupelo, MS
www.bethelroadpublications.com

Special thanks to our Street Team for all of their editorial assistance, support, and prayers. You all know who you are, and most importantly, God knows who you are! You are a blessing to the world.

For Jesus,
the Repairer of All Things Broken

*Now that which we see is as if we were looking
in a broken mirror. But then we will see everything.
Now I know only a part. But then I will know everything
in a perfect way. That is how God knows me right now.*
1 Corinthians 13:12

PROLOGUE

Kelly stood at the sink, washing the last of the remaining dirty dishes. Her heart was peaceful, her mind contemplative. Movement outside caught her attention and she looked out the window before her. She smiled as she saw Tessa walking to the swing set with the twins, Bella and Evie. From behind, Tessa looked like a normal teenage girl, full of fun and life and promise. And then she turned slightly to the side and the protruding bulge from her belly told a different story. Hers was one of heartache and trouble, mistakes and loneliness. And for just a moment, memories like an unexpected wave swept over Kelly.

The warm water poured over her hands, still grasping the dirty plate. But she didn't feel it or see it. She just stood there watching—and remembering.

Stan walked in and paused mid-step as he saw his wife's beautiful face, her expression lost in unspoken thoughts. He knew that look. Sometimes he saw that look on her face when they drove down the road together, her eyes looking straight ahead, seeing things unseen on the road. Or maybe she was seeing the road behind them. It didn't matter to him. She was his in the here and now. And in the forever places of the future.

"Whatcha' doin'?" he asked casually, not wanting to intrude on her thoughts, but wanting to be included in them.

"Look at her," she said, not taking her eyes from the scene outside the window.

Stan walked to the window and simply looked, too. Neither said a word for a full minute. Stan broke the silence and the unspoken stream of thoughts. "It was a nice night. I think she had a good time, don't you?"

"I want her to stay," Kelly said simply.

"We will have her back over to visit soon," Stan said as he put his arm around her.

She turned toward him and looked at him intently, her eyes locked on his. She paused just a moment, silently begging him to hear—really hear—her. "I want her to stay, Stan."

"What do you mean? She can't stay. We told the director we would have her back to the home by nine."

Kelly looked out the window again. She saw Tessa pushing both girls in side-by-side swings, back and forth, back and forth. She was smiling, even looked peaceful, caught up temporarily in the beautiful moment of an ordinary day in the life of an ordinary family—new territory for her.

"Stan, listen, please," Kelly said, now turning her attention back to him, willing him to understand. "She is the mother of our son. I don't want her in some *home*. I want her at *our* home."

"I don't think that would be very wise," Stan said, nervous laughter on the edge of his voice.

Kelly looked down at her still wet hands. She silently turned off the water and placed the last dish, now clean, in the dishwasher.

"Kelly, talk to me. You can't be serious. That just isn't done. It's too complicated. There are too many details and emotions to consider. You need to think of her. Will that really be the best thing for her? I mean ... after. That could get really, really hard for all of us."

Kelly looked at Stan as he spoke. She didn't say a word for several seconds. "I don't know about all that, Stan. I know people don't do that. I know our friends and family would think we were being foolish. But I don't really care. I just care about her." She paused for a moment, trying to think of a way to articulate what was forming in her mind and in her heart.

"Stan, when I look at her, I see me. It is the strangest sensation I have ever had. It's like looking in a mirror, only the mirror is a reflection of another me in another life," she said, emotion making her voice sound strange, even to her.

She paused, once again, looking intently at his face, longing for his expression to show even a glimmer of understanding. Not yet.

She looked back out at the scene before her. The twins had just jumped off the swings and Tessa was chasing them, as fast as her unbalanced body would allow. Just as they heard the doorknob of the back door twist, Kelly looked back up at the husband she adored and simply said, once again, "I want her to stay."

CHAPTER

Six-year-old Kelly looked back at her two sisters with a gloating smile. Her heart still pounded from her mad dash to the car.

"Addi may be older, but I'm faster," she thought proudly.

"We're off like a herd of turtles," her grandfather said teasingly. As he pulled out of the driveway, he turned the knob on the AM/FM radio. He paused on the local rock station just long enough to hear the first Stanza of Pink Floyd's number one hit, "Another Brick in the Wall".

We don't need no education
We don't need no thought control
No dark sarcasm in the classroom
Teachers leave them kids alone
Hey teacher leave them kids alone
All in all it's just another brick in the wall

He grunted disapprovingly and quickly turned the knob again and again finally settling on his favorite, the WAYFM Gospel station. Andrae' Crouch & The Disciples crooned their latest chorus, "I'll Be Thinking of You". Granddaddy sang along quietly, seemingly deep in thought, or prayer, or both.

It was early summer, 1979. School had dismissed a few days early, school administrators citing unused snow days. Kelly was glad. May in Mississippi was hot. The air-conditioning campaign had covered the central heat and air costs for the high school and middle school, but had not yet reached the elementary school. Kelly could still recall the buzzing of the window unit in her classroom, cooling only the lucky ones seated near the unit. Even as a first grader, Kelly knew how to fold notebook paper first to the front, then to the back, over and over until she had formed a fan to cool herself.

The hot sun poured in through the car windows, causing Kelly to wish she had her notebook paper with her. She scooted up to the edge of the seat and stuck her face directly in front of the air vent. She let the semi-cool air blow her blond hair, never thinking of the effort her mother had gone through to comb the curly locks.

She looked out the front windshield and stared at the mirage of hazy air rising ahead of her on the road. Just as it appeared that the car would catch up to the floating haze, it would disappear and she would see it further ahead on the sun-covered highway. This kept her attention for a while, but soon the warmth of the sun and the vibration of the car caused her eyes to grow heavy. She sat back and leaned against the side door, pulling her legs up on the seat and leaning her head on the window. She glanced over at her beloved grandfather. He looked at her and quickly winked before turning his gaze back to the highway.

Granddaddy was her mother's dad. He was a Methodist

preacher and boldly spoke of and lived out God's truth. He was active in their lives, living in the same small Mississippi town. Lately, Granddaddy had been around even more than usual. Her mom had been "under the weather," as the adults in her life said, though she was not quite sure what that meant.

Kelly felt sleepy, yet content and happy. She was excited to see Aunt Rose and Uncle Al. She knew they weren't really her aunt and uncle, but that is what she called them. They were college friends of her parents and she had visited their farm on a number of occasions. It was always fun, always full of adventure. Of course, she had never spent the night there before, but she wasn't scared because her sisters were with her.

This trip was arranged so that the girls would be "out of her hair," as her father, Will Humphrey, put it when Kelly overheard him talking on the phone. Her mother was going in for some tests, he had said. Kelly didn't really know what that meant, but she had gathered that it wasn't like the spelling tests she took every Friday. Apparently, you had to take these tests at the hospital.

Aunt Rose and Uncle Al lived in Alabama on a farm about three hours away. They had 600 acres of soybean fields, woods, and even a small lake. They also kept horses, which Kelly loved to ride, as long as someone pulled the reins ahead of her leading the horse in a slow, safe pace. For this visit, they would stay a whole week. She had never been away from her parents for a whole week before. She was excited, but a bit nervous, too. Aunt Rose said each one of the three girls would have their own room to stay in for the week. Her sisters, Addi, age ten, and Molly, age four, were excited about that. Addi had already informed Kelly that under no circumstances would she be allowed to sleep with either of them. She hoped she would be brave because "acting like a baby" was unthinkable.

They had only gotten a few miles down the road and already Kelly felt as if they had been driving forever. She looked at her grandfather again and said, "Are we almost there?"

He smiled and replied firmly, yet patiently, "No, Sugar, we are not almost there. The time will pass quicker if you go to sleep."

She sighed deeply and said, "Okay," drawing the sound of the letters out begrudgingly. She then leaned her head back against the window and closed her eyes and daydreamed of the fun to come until she fell asleep.

CHAPTER

2

Kelly awoke when her grandfather pulled onto the long, gravel driveway of Aunt Rose and Uncle Al's farm. She wiped the drool from her cheek and sat up on the edge of the seat, taking in the sights of the beautiful land around her. She could see the white farmhouse up ahead with its wrap around porch and red swing. Small fluttering in her stomach made her feel a bit uneasy. Was she nervous or excited? Maybe a little bit of both. Her grandfather kept driving until he was right next to the house. He pulled into a shady, grassy spot by the porch entrance. Before they were all out of the car, Aunt Rose had come outside to greet them.

"Hello, girls! I am so happy you are here," Aunt Rose said cheerfully.

Granddaddy handed each of the girls their small suitcases and Aunt Rose instructed the girls to go claim a bedroom. Addi raced upstairs, determined to claim the biggest and best bedroom, and Molly followed as closely as her little legs would allow. Kelly, still a bit drowsy from the drive, held back just a bit. She was not quite sure she was ready to leave her grandfather. She noticed that Granddaddy and Aunt Rose spoke in soft, serious tones and Kelly wondered what they were talking about. She decided to sit quietly on the porch steps and listen in on their conversation. She heard her mother's name, Sadie, and then before she could listen further, Granddaddy told her to "run along, now", which she did reluctantly. As she rose from the step where she sat, movement in the barn caught her eye. *Maybe it's Uncle Al*, she thought excitedly. He was always so nice to each of the girls, although Kelly seemed to be his favorite.

"Aunt Rose, may I go to the barn?" she asked quickly.

"Of course, dear," Aunt Rose said with a smile, which disappeared as she turned her attention back to Granddaddy.

Kelly left her suitcase on the top step, jumped down the last three, and raced to the barn. The contrast of the bright sunlight outside and the dark shadows inside the barn made Kelly stop in her tracks. She paused inside the big wooden door and waited for her eyes to adjust. Even before she could see clearly, she heard his voice.

"There she is!" Uncle Al's deep voice boomed.

Before she could even return the greeting, he had swooped her up in a big hug, which she eagerly returned. She hugged tightly and then began to pull away. But he kept hugging her. So she hugged tightly once again. Still, he kept hugging her, although the hug was softer now. She squirmed just a bit, suddenly feeling a nervous, fluttering sensation in her stomach.

Uncle Al released her and placed her solidly on the ground.

"Well, my Kelly! How are you?" he asked cheerfully.

"I'm fine," she answered shyly.

"What would you like to do first," he asked. Kelly merely shrugged her shoulders in return.

"How about I show you how to feed the horses?" he asked, a pleasant smile covering his face.

Kelly nodded and a smile covered her own face. Uncle Al held out his hand, which she took reluctantly, and they headed to the corral to see the horses.

CHAPTER

A week later, Kelly stood at the front window of the farmhouse. Rain poured down from the black clouds above. The great sheets fell like a curtain, blocking her view of the long, gravel driveway. Still, she strained her eyes to see what she had longed to see for the past five days.

Where is Granddaddy? she thought frantically. *He said he would be here by nine.*

Her eyes held fast to the scene outside when suddenly the sheet of rain turned into an imaginary movie screen as scenes from the past week came unbidden to her memory. These scenes were dark and ugly and scary. Kelly was not really sure they had happened. She was confused as images of dark shadows in the middle of the night took over her mind leaving her no other choice but to relive them. Pain and shame threatened to suffocate her. Fear like a vice grip squeezed her heart and soul as she wondered if he would follow through on his threats.

Where is Granddaddy? she thought once again as her heart pounded in her little chest. *He will know what to do,* the thought slowing the rhythm of her heart only slightly.

Suddenly, she heard heavy footsteps coming down the stairs from the darkness of the bedrooms. She had tried her best to run from those steps in the waking hours. At night she had tried to fall asleep quickly for Granddaddy had said, "The time will pass quicker if you go to sleep."

Only he was wrong this time, because the time was endless, even when she slept. The nightmares made the time pass at a snail's place and the line between what was a nightmare and what was real had become fuzzy and unrecognizable to her young mind. As the footsteps got closer, she thought she might scream or, at the very least, finally let the suppressed tears loose like a raging flood. She cowered behind the curtain, glancing outside once again longing to see the blue Cadillac come up the driveway. With white knuckles, her hand grasped her suitcase, and she let out a cry as she saw a hint of blue through the curtain of rain. *Granddaddy!* She took off immediately flying out the door and into the storm, glad once again she could run fast.

Having gotten to the car first, she had the front seat next to Granddaddy on the ride home. She scooted as close to him as possible, feeling only slight relief. *Maybe if I tell him, I will feel better, safer,* she thought. She scooted even closer to him as she tried to think of a way to share her nightmare. Just as she was about to speak, Granddaddy cleared his throat the way he always did when he had something important to say.

"Girls, I need to talk to you. Your mama went in for some tests this week," he paused and cleared his throat once again. As Kelly looked at Granddaddy's face, she detected tears glistening in his wrinkled eyes. He definitely had their attention.

"Your mama is sick. And she is not going to get better," he said bluntly.

"Is she going to die?" Addi asked from the backseat.

"Well, we all are going to die," he replied. "But I don't think your mama is going to die anytime soon. But her life is going to be different now. She won't be able to do things for you anymore. She will do much better if you are all good and don't cause her any stress. You've got to help her. Do you hear me?"

"Yes, sir," both sisters in the back said in unison.

Granddaddy looked over at Kelly with his sad, serious eyes and awaited her answer.

"Yes, sir," she said quietly, as she scooted back toward the passenger window, determined to keep her nightmare to herself. For if she told anyone, her mama might die.

CHAPTER

4

Fourteen-year-old Kelly hopped off the school bus in front of her house. *First day of high school! Things are looking up now,* she thought cheerfully. She took the key out of the side pocket of her backpack and opened the door to the kitchen. Her eyes fell on the dirty dishes in the sink. *I should have done those last night*, she thought guiltily. *Okay, here's the plan. I will check on Mom, then start supper. I'll just wait and wash all the dishes at once*, she thought.

"Mom! I'm home!" she yelled from the kitchen. She grabbed an apple from the sparse contents of the refrigerator, slid her backpack off her back and dropped it on the kitchen table. *I better get started on my homework, after I start a load of laundry,* she thought, her to-do list for the evening growing longer.

Other kids her age didn't have to do the kinds of things she had to do, but she didn't really mind. Well, most of the time she didn't mind. Occasionally though, she longed for the kind of life she saw her friends living. Oh, they complained, but they just didn't know. Kelly always kept quiet when they complained, especially when they complained about their moms. But inside, she boiled. She wanted to scream at them,

Get over yourselves! You don't even know what you've got! But she never did. She just changed the subject or made a joke. That was usually her strategy. Just laugh it away. It's nobody's business anyway.

"Mom?" she called as she walked down the hall toward the master bedroom. She paused at the door to see if her mother was sleeping. She wasn't. She smiled slightly when she saw Kelly, the right side of her cheek rising higher than the left.

Kelly couldn't really remember what life was like before her mom got sick. Every once in a while she had a vague memory of her mom's gentle push against her back as she swung back and forth in the swing in the backyard. The swing set was still there, but it was rusted and broken and surrounded by weeds. Her dad did the best he could in keeping up with the yard, doing the housework and taking care of Kelly, Addi, and Molly, but with his full time job at Reed's Department Store and the full time job of taking care of her mom, he didn't have much time or energy for the other things. Kelly and Addi long ago took over the laundry and cooking duties, and now that Addi was off at college, it fell on Kelly to help her dad and look after Molly. But, though she realized her life was not "normal" it was the only life she knew.

When her mom was diagnosed with Multiple Sclerosis, or MS as everyone called it, none of them knew exactly how it would change their lives. Little by little they had adjusted to a new normal, with their dear caretaker now in need of care. It was terribly hard on all of them, especially seeing their beloved mother slowly lose the use of her legs and then her arms. Now the muscles in her face and neck had begun to deteriorate, making smiles and laughter and long conversations more and more difficult.

MS. Such a short term for such a long illness. MS is a

chronic autoimmune disease that affects the central nervous system. The cause is unknown and there is no cure. The damage caused by MS creates scars called lesions that can be seen on the brain, spinal cord, and optic nerve. Because the process of developing these lesions is called sclerosis, multiple sclerosis literally means "many scars"—the understatement of the century, in so many ways.

Some people with MS have minimal symptoms, well-controlled with medicine. Not so for Sadie. She had been diagnosed with chronic progressive MS, which meant she never found a state of remission. Over the years her family stood by helplessly watching her body fail.

It began with fatigue and back pain, and quickly progressed into the numbness of her extremities and paralysis. She had gone from outgoing and energetic to bedridden and totally dependent. Her dependence, however, was not just on her family. Her real dependence was on her God.

"Hey, Mom. How was your day?" Kelly asked, just as she always did.

"Okay," her mother answered, giving her standard reply.

"Will you help me, Kel?" she asked, vulnerable eyes searching those of her middle daughter.

"Sure, Mom. What can I get for you?"

"I need to go to the bathroom," she answered, slightly embarrassed. Lately, Sadie had lost some more milestones, including the strength of muscles around her bladder. This was humiliating to her and she still had not accepted this aspect of her disease.

"Mom, Dad will be home soon. Can you wait just a little bit longer?" she asked, compassion pulling at her heart, yet knowing what her dad had told her. *Let me help her. She is too heavy for you. You could hurt her if you're not careful."*

The family had settled into a routine which worked—at least most of the time. Her father woke up early and tended to the immediate needs of his wife. He made sure his girls ate breakfast and were ready for the school bus at 7:15. He then bathed and dressed Sadie, made sure she was fed, comfortable and that the phone, remote control, and her Bible were close by, and then went to work. He came home at ten to check on her and attend to her needs, and then again at noon to fix lunch for her. He came again at three and was home by five to attend to his wife and parent his children.

Will was thankful for his job at Reed's. Founded in 1905, Reed's was a family owned and operated business. The department store was located in downtown Tupelo and was housed in a beautiful brick building, symbolic of its strong foundation and enduring presence in the community. The concept of family was strong at Reed's, and this concept extended to non-family employees like Will Humphrey. They supported him in dealing with his unique family situation, and in turn they received loyalty and hard work which went beyond the normal employer-employee relationship.

"Mom, Dad will be home soon. Can you wait?"

She looked away from Kelly and shook her head, "No."

"Okay, Mom. We can do this!" Kelly said over-cheerfully, trying to ease her mom's embarrassment.

Kelly walked to the corner of the room and pushed her mother's wheelchair to the side of the bed. She then pulled the covers off of her mom and slid both hands gently under her calves. She knew she must be very careful, because her bones were so brittle, they could break without warning. She gently pulled her mother's body until she was horizontal on the bed. She reached forward and placed one arm under her back and the other under her knees. She gently lifted her mother like a baby and strained to move her toward the wheelchair.

Suddenly, her mother's immobile foot got caught on the arm of the wheelchair, causing Kelly to lose her balance. She tried to balance herself, but without use of her arms, she stumbled landing on her back. Subconsciously, she had guarded her mother's frail body to the best of her ability, and took the brunt of the fall on herself. They both screamed as they hit the ground.

Tears fell down Kelly's cheeks as she assessed the damage to her mom, ignoring her own pain.

"Mom! Are you okay? I'm so sorry! What hurts?" she asked, panic rising with every word. "Mom! Speak to me! Are you okay?"

With a glazed look in her eyes, her mother looked frightened and wounded. She just looked at her daughter and then tears fell from her own eyes. Still, she said nothing.

Kelly placed her mom as gently as she could on the floor and began to search her arms and legs, looking for protruding bones. She saw none. And yet, what did she know? She was only fourteen.

"Mom, I have to call Dad," Kelly said frantically.

"No," her mom said as firmly as her weak voice could manage.

"But, Mom, please … I'm so scared you are hurt."

"You help," her mom said with tears still spilling from her eyes, yet unable to wipe them away.

Kelly looked at her mom for several seconds, with tears still pouring from her own eyes. She wanted to respect her mom, to obey her. She wanted even more to restore the dignity her mom had just lost, and had continually lost for eight long years.

"Okay. I'll try," she said reluctantly.

Kelly gently tried to lift her mom off the floor. Sadie cried out in pain as she did. Kelly laid her back on the floor and weeping, said, "I'm sorry, Mom. I have to call him." She got up and ran from the room to retrieve the phone.

Thirty minutes later, she sat at the kitchen table, staring out the window. Her father walked in the room and sat across from her. She looked up and saw anger in his eyes.

"Is she okay?" she asked, tears forming again in her still red eyes.

"Yes," he said.

"I'm sorry, Dad. I knew better, but …" she couldn't finish the sentence without sounding like she was making excuses. "I'm just sorry," she said simply.

"I know she put pressure on you to do that; she told me the whole story. I know you were just trying to respect her. But you have to believe me when I say you have to listen to me in situations like that. Your mom … she just …" he paused, trying to express his thoughts.

"Before your mom got sick, she was so … full of life. So independent. So energetic. It's really, really hard for her to accept how she is now, because that is not really her. She still feels the same on the inside, but her outside won't cooperate. So, sometimes she wants to buck the system. She wants to pretend she can, when she can't. It's up to us to help her during those times. To help her see that we still see the old her, but at the same time protect her when she needs it. Do you understand?"

Kelly nodded and looked down at her hands. She paused a

moment before she spoke. "Dad?"

"Yeah, Baby?"

"Tell me more about her ... before. I don't remember. Every now and then I get these brief flashes in my mind. I think I remember what it was like, but then I wonder if maybe it's not really a memory—maybe I am just making up a happy thought from things I have seen on TV or at my friends' houses. Maybe I am imagining what I wish was real."

Her Dad smiled a sad smile which didn't quite reach his eyes, and reached across the table and took Kelly's hands in his. "Your mother," he began, "was the Belle of the Ball. She was beautiful. I fell in love with her when I saw her as the captain of the cheerleading squad. She loved her friends so much. We used to host great parties. She was a friend to everyone. It didn't matter who they were or what their background was. She just loved people with this special energy that lifted them up." He paused as if he were suddenly reliving former days, ordinary at the time, but now considered quite extraordinary.

"She and I used to work with the youth group at the church. Do you remember that?"

"Yes. I remember I couldn't wait to get old enough for youth group. I would watch y'all and you both were so fun and all the teenagers loved you. I remember being proud that you were my parents."

"I'm sorry we couldn't do that for you, Kelly. You have no idea how much we both wish we could," he said sadly. "We don't talk about it much. I guess we all just have realized it is what it is and there is nothing we can do to change it. And maybe we think if we talk about it, the pain will hurt worse. But I want you to know we both realize how much you have lost to this disease. It has taken your away your privilege of being 'mothered'. I wish it wasn't so."

Rather than take the opportunity to share her hurts and mourn her loss, Kelly did what she thought would be less painful for her parents—she ran from the truth of it all and the raw emotion of it.

"It's okay, Dad. I promise." She then rose from the table and went to start a load of laundry before she began cooking dinner for herself and her family.

CHAPTER

Will slowly rose from the table and walked out into the backyard. As his mother used to say, Mississippi was hot as Hades in August. Just walking across the yard made streams of sweat run down the sides of his face. *At least these aren't tears*, he thought, though they could have been. He sure felt like crying.

The walk down memory lane was more painful than he would have ever admitted to Kelly. Sure, it was bittersweet, but at this moment, the bitter outweighed the sweet. He felt the weight of loss in a way that came only occasionally. Most of the time he was too busy to think about what he had lost—what Sadie and the girls had lost. Most of the time he just accepted life as it had been given to him.

However, now and then he gave himself the freedom to remember and to grieve. This was one of those times. As he walked around in the yard, pretending to check the weed-filled flower beds, he remembered. Bitter memories and sweet memories both flew through his mind in haphazard fashion.

Scenes of Sadie in high school and college, parties and dates, friends and laughter all flashed through his mind. He saw Sadie in her long, flowing gown walking down the fifty yard line with the other girls on the Homecoming Court. She was the prettiest one out there—at least to him.

He saw her running round and round the track, as he cheered her on to win the race at the regional track meet. She still was running a race of sorts, and he was still cheering her on.

His mind traveled back in time to the day they knew something was wrong. Their busy schedule had prevented a home cooked meal that night, so she headed to the local McDonald's. As she approached a stop sign, she tried to press on the brake, but her foot wouldn't move. Mentally, she tried again to move her foot, even envisioned it moving, but physically, her body wouldn't cooperate. In seconds, she knew, as did Addi who was riding in the front passenger's seat, that something was terribly wrong. The sound of the crash into the car in front of her screamed the unwelcome truth.

Choosing happier memories, he thought of the day he asked her to marry him. Young, college graduates, they sat for hours dreaming of the future and of all the happy moments that were sure to come. And happy moments did come. Those early years were filled with laughter and joy. Sadie always had an ample supply of both. She was strong-willed and independent and so much fun. Even when she was first diagnosed, they still chose laughter.

Another memory flashed across his mind taking him back to those early days of their journey with MS. They had decided to take the girls to Opryland, the fun, country music theme park in Nashville. He tried to get her to ride in a wheelchair, but she would have none of that. They had all tried to walk slowly—without her realizing it, of course—but keeping up with the girls youthful enthusiasm made them all forget. That is until she fell. That was the first of many falls.

After he had confirmed she wasn't hurt other than a scrape or two, they sat in silence together on the sidewalk. Even the girls just sat. No one said a word for several seconds, until Sadie broke the silence with an uproar of laughter. This type of laughter was what he really missed—the belly-aching, tears-streaming laughter. After the laughter had faded, she looked at him, eyes still shining and said, "I would rather laugh than cry."

Me, too, he thought. Though her weak muscles made a good belly-laugh near impossible, she could still smile. And that was exactly what he needed to see right now.

He reached down and picked one of the last of the gardenia blooms. He brought it close to his face, breathing in the sweet smell.

That ought to do it, he thought. And then he turned to take his beautiful bride something to make her smile, which of course, would make him smile, too.

CHAPTER

6

Three years later, Kelly pulled her old, blue Chevy out of the driveway. It wasn't the greatest car for sure, but she was grateful to have something to drive. She was definitely surprised when she got a car on the day she got her driver's license, but her dad said it would make it easier on everyone. She spent lots of time in the car now, taking Molly to and from school, dance class, and church activities, not to mention keeping up with her own activities.

For the past two years she had enjoyed running track. It was a short season and she could manage it along with her other responsibilities. Plus, it made her happy to be able to share that common interest with her mom. Of course, her mom couldn't even walk now, much less run, but she could remember what it was like and it seemed to give her pleasure to reminisce.

Presently, Kelly was headed to deliver photos from the spring dance to her friend, Jill. As she drove down the street in the quiet neighborhood, Kelly sang along as U2 belted out "I Still Haven't Found What I'm Looking For" from the blaring radio. Kelly could relate. It seemed lately, as much as she tried, she couldn't ease the discontentment she felt. The feeling seemed to pounce out of nowhere at the oddest times. It felt as if she was longing for something she had lost, though what that was she couldn't say. Sometimes she just wanted to run. It didn't matter where. She just wanted to get away from the dark cloud which seemed to follow her around.

As the song ended, the DJ's clear voice announced the call letters, WTBJ-Classic Rock, and proudly introduced "a blast from the not so distant past by Pink Floyd." The initial notes had a familiar sound and Kelly listened closely to see if she could guess the song.

> *We don't need no education*
> *We don't need no thought control*
> *No dark sarcasm in the classroom*
> *Teachers leave them kids alone*
> *Hey teacher leave them kids alone*
> *All in all it's just another brick in the wall*

As she listened her way through the first stanza, her heart began to race, and sweat appeared on her forehead. She felt slightly dizzy. *What's wrong with me?* she asked herself in the fog of sudden anxiety. A scene flashed in her mind, bringing with it a thorough covering of darkness, as if a dark cloud had suddenly dampened a sunny day. The warm summer light streaming in the window mocked her depressed state, bringing realization that the darkness was in her alone, not in the world around her. She shook her head in an effort to shake away the unwelcome memory. She quickly changed the radio station and turned the air conditioning vent directly on her still sweating face. *Get a grip, Kelly,* she thought to herself as she turned onto the quiet street where Jill lived.

After a short visit, with plans for a night out with friends now firmly in place, Kelly got back into her car to head back home. *If I'm going to be able to go out tonight, I'd better be sure that supper is ready first.* She reached over and turned off the radio, unwilling to risk another anxiety attack.

At the end of Jill's street, Kelly stopped at the four-way stop. She then inched forward just a bit, trying to see around the blooming hedge which had grown too full with its summer growth. The way was clear and she began to turn left. Suddenly, a car appeared, seemingly out of nowhere. Kelly screamed as the realization came that she was going to be hit. She closed her eyes and braced herself for the crash. The impact sent her car spinning. The sound of metal to metal and rubber to pavement echoed in the silence of the quiet neighborhood.

As her car came to a stop in a neighboring yard, Kelly struggled to breathe. *God, I can't breathe,* she thought frantically. *Breathe, Kelly,* she spoke silently to herself. *Stay calm; it's going to be okay.*

As her head cleared and her breathing slowed, her surroundings suddenly came back into focus. She then realized that though she was still buckled into the driver's seat, the location of that seat was now on top of the passenger's side. The roof of the car was pointing upward, as if beckoning to the only Source of help. The front windows and the windshield were completely shattered, and glass shards stung her arms and her face. But she barely felt their sting, for a pain much greater demanded her attention.

At the time of the collision, Kelly's left knee leaned comfortably against the door. The impact of the wreck pushed her femur through her pelvic girdle, shattering the left side of her pelvis. As the shock of the wreck wore off, the pain increased and she cried out for help. She tried to sit up, but realized she couldn't move her legs. She could hear sirens in the background as she once again struggled to breathe. As the sirens got closer and closer, their sound in her ears grew more and more faint, until she could neither hear nor see anything and fell willingly into the darkness enveloping her.

Kelly could hear voices around her and could feel movement beneath her, though she knew she was lying down. A radio sounded in the background, only this one did not have melodies pouring from it, just scratchy sounds with facts and information flying back and forth. She opened her eyes to see a man above her adjusting a tube that stuck in her arm.

"What?" she asked, though she couldn't seem to form any other words.

"You're okay. We are on the way to the hospital. You were in a wreck," the man replied, seeming to perfectly understand her limited questioning.

"I'll call your mom for you. What's her name?"

"No, call my dad," she managed to reply. "Will Humphrey. He works at Reed's Department Store." With that last statement, the darkness beckoned again, and again she willingly surrendered to that painless place.

CHAPTER

7

Days later, she lay in the hospital bed staring at the ceiling. She fought the urge to cry. She had learned over the years crying didn't change anything. Pain shot through her leg causing her to grit her teeth and squeeze her eyes shut, as a lone tear fell from the corners of her eyes. After a moment, it subsided only slightly. It seemed to come in waves like the ocean, only these waves were not calm. They were rough and dangerous and scary, and they threatened to overwhelm her. When the wave of pain subsided slightly, she turned her head to the left and saw her dad dozing in the chair beside her. His head cocked unnaturally to the right, and Kelly knew he would be in pain himself when he woke up.

Who's with mom? she suddenly thought, panic rising. The fact that the roles were at times reversed, went unnoticed and unacknowledged. She took care of her mom, because her mom could not take care of herself, not to mention Kelly or her sisters. There was no resentment toward her mom for this reality. It simply was. Kelly knew her mom would give anything to be the one in the chair beside her.

Kelly had spoken once on the phone to her mom since

the accident. When that conversation had occurred, she didn't really know. Time seemed endless as the shadows of the light outside came brightly in the window, then faded persistently and consistently. She lost track of time and now marked its passing by nurse visits and pain medication. She didn't really remember what her mother had said, as the pain medication was finally taking effect when they spoke. She did recall that her mother was crying, and Kelly felt such compassion for her, knowing how painful it was for her to be unable to be with her.

Another wave of pain caught Kelly off guard and she winced loudly. Her father stirred suddenly and sat up quickly. "Are you, okay?" he said anxiously. She nodded slightly and tried to hide her pain, just as she had done for as long as she could remember.

"Is it almost time for my pain meds?" she asked.

"I will go check," he said, rising quickly. He walked out of the room stiffly, rubbing his neck.

How many days has it been? she thought. *And he has not left my side*, she realized suddenly. Once again, she thought, *Who's with mom?*

Her dad returned shortly and said sympathetically, "The nurse said you still have two hours before the next dose."

Kelly just looked at him for a moment, until a wave of pain rose once again, and she shut her eyes against its flood. Her own internal flood then came, and she could no longer hold back her tears. She cried loud and long, and her father stood helplessly beside her, holding her hand and sweeping back her hair. If she had not been so lost in her own pain, she would have seen another stream of tears falling from his eyes.

"I'll be right back, Honey," he said as he quickly left the room.

He returned quickly, with the nurse in tow.

"Kelly, I am going to add a different medication to your IV," she said calmly. "This one should help with your pain until you can have another dose of the Percocet. Opioid analgesics are prescribed for moderate to severe pain, and are used in step two and step three of the analgesic ladder. Dependence and tolerance are well-known features with regular use, so you and your parents will have to be aware of that."

Kelly sobbed even louder as tears of relief mixed with tears of pain. "Thank you," she managed to mumble as the nurse added a needle filled with a clear liquid to the IV tube and then clamped it closed again.

Three weeks later, Kelly sat up in the hospital bed with a tray on her lap. Her leg still hung in traction, but she was able to at least hold the tray and watch a little television now. They had finally found a good combination of pain meds to keep the constant pain from overwhelming her mind and emotions. Her dad finally felt comfortable leaving her side, and deep down she was happy to have the small room to herself. She also felt less worried about her mom, now that her dad could leave and check on her, which is where he was now.

The thick, boxy television hung precariously from a shelf high in the west corner of the room. Kelly glanced up just as Blossom laid out a ridiculous line. How this show was so popular, Kelly would never understand, though she did find herself smiling a time or two and despite her annoyance, she didn't bother to change the channel. The storyline about a teenage girl living in an unconventional family seemed relatable somehow, especially when Blossom, the main character, dreamed of what life would be like in a more "normal" family.

Kelly had the same thoughts at times. No, she would never want to change the characters in her story. She just would change the storyline. In a perfect story, Kelly would be at home now, not in a hospital bed. And instead of hospital food, she would be sitting at the table eating a home-cooked meal, lovingly prepared by her mother. They would sit and laugh and talk about their day, and there would be homemade dessert every night. Kelly smiled to herself at the silly thoughts.

Well, I can dream, she thought. Suddenly, like a freight train out of nowhere, the dark shadow of evil memories ran over her. Her heart pounded in her chest and sweat broke out on her brow, and though she bid it to stay away, the thought persisted in her mind. *In a perfect story, little girls are not wounded and scarred by trusted grown men*, she thought miserably. In all the passing years, Kelly had never told anyone what had happened that summer so long ago.

She suddenly lost her appetite and pushed back the tray of cold meatloaf and watery mashed potatoes. *I think I will ask for another pain pill*, she thought suddenly, knowing that the medicine would ease the persistent pain in her leg, as well as cover the pain of her soul in a cloud of fluffy forgetfulness—even if just for a little while.

She reached for the bulky remote control attached to the wall and lying at the top of her mattress. After she called the nurse, she pressed the power button off and watched as the picture faded to a tiny dot in the center of the screen of the outdated television. She stared at the dot until it, too, faded into the darkness of the screen. She lay back on the pillow and closed her eyes, waiting on the medicine. She fought the nagging feeling that she really didn't need the pain meds as much as she wanted the pain meds. *Well, I deserve it,* she thought. *Maybe I can take a nap when they give me more medicine.*

Suddenly, she felt very tired. Tired and old beyond her years. She was weary of the fight and though she willed the tears away, one lone tear slid out of the corner of her eye. She didn't bother to wipe it away until she heard the door to her room open.

"Hey, Kelly," a male voice said, just as a sandy-haired, blue-eyed face appeared around the door.

Kelly looked up and saw the familiar face of her friend, Chris. Chris lived two hours away, but they had developed a friendship over the years which had begun at a Junior High church retreat. They continued to water the seeds of friendship each spring when they competed on opposing school track teams. Kelly viewed him simply as a friend, however she always wondered if the seeds of friendship might one day bloom into something more. Without thought, she reached up and combed her fingers through her dirty hair, regretting that she had declined the morning nurse's offer to wash it for her.

Kelly sat up as best she could and quickly responded with a wide smile. "What are you doing here?" she asked.

"I had to check on my track buddy. I heard about your wreck. I'm really sorry. Are you in a lot of pain?" As he spoke he slowly approached the hospital bed and reached out to gently tuck a runaway strand of hair behind her ear. For some reason, the gentleness of that action made Kelly want to cry.

She looked down to avoid his gaze and replied, "Well, yeah,

this has been pretty painful, but the medicine helps."

"Will I get to cheer you on in track this year?" he asked hopefully.

"I don't think so. The doctor says I have probably a year of recovery ahead of me. And even then, he doesn't think my leg will be the same as it was before."

"I'm sorry," he said, still trying to catch her eye.

She looked up and saw the gentleness and sincerity in his eyes, and suddenly felt a new emotion. She felt cherished. She smiled at him and replied.

"Thanks. Me, too," she simply said. "Want to watch some TV with me?"

"Sure," he replied with a smile. He sat in the chair next to her bed and propped his legs gently on her mattress, careful not to move it. They sat in comfortable silence and watched the end of Blossom, laughing together at the silly antics.

CHAPTER

8

Kelly slowly managed to get into the front seat of Jill's new Lexus LS400. An early graduation present, this new Toyota luxury car had all the bells and whistles. Kelly tried hard not to be jealous. She knew she would never have a car this nice. *Well, she is going to be a grade-A sorority girl at Ole Miss, so I guess it fits.* Kelly felt guilty as soon as the thought entered her mind. Jill had been nothing but nice to her. But with all the medical bills in the past year, divided between Kelly and Sadie, Will would not be able to buy a new car for Kelly's graduation as he had hoped. When she was able to drive again, she would go off to Mississippi State in a sensible used car. They were lucky they had good car insurance when hers was totaled during the wreck. *That is, if I graduate,* Kelly thought. As it stood now, she might not get to hobble across the stage and shake hands with the high school principal to receive her diploma. She had missed so much school due to her injuries, and now she was very far behind. Her guidance counselor was working very hard to help her. In fact, the care she felt from Mrs. Levin was like a cool drink on a hot summer day. Mrs. Levin had personally spoken with all of her teachers and had arranged tutoring sessions after school most days. Not that she had other school activities to occupy her. She had been forced to give up track and had missed signing up for any other club or event because of her rehab schedule. *Not the senior year I had hoped for,* she often thought. All in all, she was simply ready for high school to be over. A new start is what she needed.

    Several of her friends, and even Mrs. Levin, had stepped up to help take Kelly to and from school, as well as to the biweekly rehab sessions Kelly was still attending. Yes, her leg had improved. However, it still hurt and the medicine helped with that hurt as well as the deeper hurt Kelly tried desperately to hide. And so it was, Kelly went through her senior year limping through a muddled fog of pain and pain relief. She also had found another form of relief, which she managed to hide from her parents. The meds mixed with the clear liquid hidden in the top of her closet seemed to make all pain cease—at least for a while. She had chosen vodka as her drink of choice because it was clear and odorless and could be mixed in with just about any drink she wanted. Her favorite combo was vodka and Dr. Pepper. Her parents did not have a clue and she was sure her friends would never tell. The ones who knew were doing the same thing, so if they ratted her out, they would be doing the same to themselves. At first, Kelly found herself having trouble sleeping as she fought the battle with her guilty conscience. But a pain pill usually solved that problem, although they didn't seem to work quite as well now, ten months after the accident.

    "Thanks for the ride," Kelly said. And she really meant it. *The beauty of a small town,* she thought. Her dad frequently said that and she agreed. Tupelo, Mississippi, was a sleepy little community where friends were like family and "do unto others" was a motto to live by. Everyone attended church, which was the social hub of the community. Kelly and her family were members of First United Methodist Church. Established in 1899 by nine devoted souls, FUMC was the oldest church in Tupelo. It had survived the great tornado of 1936, and its aged red brick and colorful stain glass set the stage for a traditional liturgical service enhanced by the organ, the hand bells, and the scheduled ringing of the large bell in the tower. Both of Kelly's parents grew up in that church, and Will still made sure his girls were there every Sunday and Wednesday night, even though Sadie had not been able to attend in several years.

In the early years, before illness and injury had robbed them all of so much, Will and Sadie were the cute, spunky couple who made sure their three girls were growing in the grace and knowledge of the Lord Jesus. They were the quintessential church volunteers, offering their youthful energy and enthusiasm to the choir, the youth group, and the Sunday school department. Will had once said to Kelly that when Sadie had to give up her service to the church, it was a great sacrifice indeed. But instead of wallowing in deserved self-pity, Sadie had determined all the more to serve God in any way possible. She dictated countless letters of encouragement, which Will patiently transcribed. She prayed fervently for many hours a day, going boldly to the throne of grace on behalf of her friends and family. She also memorized scripture after scripture until she knew first hand what Jesus meant when He said, "Man shall not live on bread alone, but on every word that comes from the mouth of God." Indeed,

Sadie feasted on the Word of God, and this was her secret strength.

Their small community was a blessing to Kelly and her family. Even though Kelly felt far away from the early faith of her childhood, she still believed that God sent little blessings along the way, and she was grateful. She didn't want to get too close to the Creator, however, for then she would have to address the many questions she had in her mind and heart, most of which began with WHY? If she dwelt on the Why questions of her heart, she would grow angry at the world, especially at God. She didn't seem to have the energy to be angry with the Creator of the Universe, so she just kept her distance.

When Kelly entered the quiet house, she made her way back to her parents' bedroom, as she did each time she came home. At times she was tempted to go straight to her room, like many of her friends did. Kelly, however, knew her mom needed contact with the outside world, and so she forced herself to sit and share every detail of her day—well, almost every detail of her day, at least the details that were happy or funny or confined to grades and rehab sessions. The ones which were difficult or dark were stuffed deep inside, though at times she was afraid they would one day bubble over like a Coke can shaken too hard. A sticky mess was to be avoided at all costs, lest the overflow further stain the brokenness of her once vivacious family.

"Hey, Mom. How was your day?" Kelly asked cheerfully.

Sadie smiled her crooked smile and slowly looked up at her beautiful daughter. *My, she is grown. Sometimes that takes my breath away,* Sadie thought wistfully. *I can't believe she is about to leave. What are we going to do without her?* Sadly, that question was racked with emotional as well as practical implications. If there was anything good that had come from Kelly's accident, it was the slow release of their reliance upon Kelly. Since Addi had left home four years ago, Kelly had been the one to keep things running smoothly in the household. Even before she could drive, it was Kelly who provided the routine that Molly had needed. In the past months, though, Kelly had not been able to keep things running, and both Will and Sadie had suddenly realized with regret she should never have been in that position anyway. *What's past is past*, Sadie thought with sadness, and deep down she knew they had all just done the best they could with the hand they had been dealt.

"It was a good day for me," Sadie responded slowly. "How about you?" she asked. She lay back on the pillow to listen. They both knew the routine. Sadie had only the strength to ask a few questions and make a few comments. It was up to Kelly to fill in the silence and keep up the conversation and the connection they felt through it. And so, Kelly began and walked her mother through the details of her day. She tried hard to add description and color to her dialog, as she knew this was one of the highlights in the endless drudgery that was her mother's life. *And yet she never complains,* Kelly often thought and reflected. *I want to be just like her when I grow up.* This sentiment had begun early in Kelly's life and had continued through her troubled teen years. Of course, she hoped and prayed she never lived a life like her mother endured, but she hoped for Sadie's spirit, and her courage, as she faced her own future.

Will scooted in close to his wife on the bed. He had fed the girls and cleaned the kitchen, and now settled in for their nightly chat. He leaned into her and kissed her soft lips and then settled comfortably against the headboard. He took Sadie's hand and gently rubbed the top of it with his thumb. *She has always had the softest skin*, he thought. She turned her head towards him and he was captured once again by her crystal blue eyes. Even after all of her suffering, her eyes still shone with love. *I am so blessed she said yes to me*, he thought once again. Even with all they had muddled through, he could not imagine life without her. He would have still wanted her, even if he had known what the future held. *I am glad I didn't know,* he thought. *Not that it would have changed things. But if I had known the difficulties of these years, the early years would not have been as joyous and carefree. I'm glad we lived well during those years when we could. I'm glad we didn't waste them.*

After a moment of comfortable silence, Sadie carefully spoke. "How's Kelly?" she asked.

Will saw her eyes change as a wave of worry passed over. He knew without more words what she was asking. They'd had this discussion several times recently. Intuitively, they both knew she was struggling. They suspected she was handling her pain in the way many teens did—and that is why they were worried. Though they did not have proof, they felt sure deep within that she was in a precarious situation. Stifled pain often led to unwise decisions, which caused more pain. They hoped this was not Kelly's story, but they were not oblivious to that possibility.

"I think she needs to get through the next few months. I'm

sorry she has had a rotten senior year. I hope and pray her college experience will be better."

"Me, too," Sadie said. The worry she felt stayed and even grew. *I can only pray*, she thought sadly. *And yet, that is the most powerful thing I could ever do.* As she continued to savor Will's tender touch, she closed her eyes and handed her worries and her daughter to the One who would not disappoint.

CHAPTER

Jill honked the car horn several times in rapid succession. She had agreed to take Kelly to an appointment, and was running late. Kelly came out the door and hurried as quickly as her leg would allow. She got into the passenger side of the Lexus and buckled her seat belt. In the past, a seat belt may have been "uncool". After what she had been through, Kelly didn't care how cool it was. She wore her seat belt at all times.

"Sorry I'm late," Jill said as she pulled away from the curb.

"That's okay. I am just thankful you could take me," Kelly replied as she dug through her purse in search of a pain pill. She opened the child-proof bottle with expert speed and popped the pill without water. She shook the bottle and then peered inside to count how many pills were left. *Only two*, she thought as her anxiety level began to rise. *Good thing I was able to get in so quickly with Dr. Roberts.*

"Doesn't your dad have to be with you for a doctor's appointment?" Jill asked.

"Not anymore. I'm eighteen now. Besides, he is working. And of course my mom ...." She left the obvious unsaid.

The truth was her parents didn't even know she had an

appointment. They had suddenly begun acting strangely about her medicine. It seemed as if they watched her like a hawk, checking to see how many pills were taken and when they were consumed. They had gone so far as to say they would not allow her to get any more Percocet. But they just didn't understand. She needed them. Her pain was still great and the anxiety she felt without the pills was not worth it.

When they arrived, Jill sat in the waiting room with Kelly as they both thumbed through a magazine. Jill looked over at her friend with concern. Kelly looked pale and sickly. Perspiration beads covered her forehead in a shimmery glow.

"Are you okay," Jill whispered with concern.

"Yes, just hurting," Kelly replied.

"But I saw you take that pill. Didn't that help?" Jill asked.

"It helped a little, but not enough. Since I have been running low, I have tried to cut back a bit. Usually, I take two. But today I only took one. I guess I needed more."

At that moment the nurse called Kelly back to an exam room and began taking her history as soon as Kelly sat down. The nurse asked very detailed questions, including the nature of her accident, how long she had been on the pain medication, and how much she took each day. It felt like an interrogation. She began to justify the continued use of her meds by describing the intense pain she experienced. The nurse took copious notes and simply nodded at Kelly's responses. She then left her alone until returning to assist Dr. Roberts.

"Hello, Kelly. I'm Dr. Roberts," he said as he extended his hand to her.

"I'm Kelly," she replied, then was suddenly embarrassed that of course he already knew her name. *Why am I so nervous,* she thought. And yet, if she were honest with herself, she knew the answer to that question. She wanted more medicine. She needed more medicine. And she was worried he would not agree to write a prescription for her.

He read through her history report and then examined her leg and pelvis, all the while asking questions about her accident, her hospital stay, her rehabilitation progress, and the frequency of her use of pain medication.

After the examination, he left the room and then returned to consult with her. He sat on the stool, while she sat upright on the examination table. His eyes spoke volumes as he looked seriously and intently at her.

"Kelly, I have examined your leg and pelvis and I do understand why you are still in pain. Unfortunately, that pain may remain for a few more months, but the good news is that I believe you will make a full recovery. The bad news is that I believe you have another problem, which we must address." He paused to take a deep breath before continuing and when he spoke again, he spoke more slowly and more carefully.

"I am sure you were warned when you were in the hospital that Percocet can be very addictive. You have long passed the time frame in which continued use is healthy. I have noticed you are a bit pale and sweaty. This is most likely due to the Percocet misuse. I know you did not mean to misuse the medicine, but I believe that is what is happening," he paused to give her time to respond, but she kept silent.

"You must get off of the Percocet, and I will not lie to you … it won't be easy or pleasant. But I will be glad to help you and give you all the support and information I can to help you with this process."

"But I need it," Kelly managed to say quietly. Her eyes

were pleading. Though he looked at her with compassion, she realized his mind was made up. *I will just go to another doctor,* she thought.

As if he could read her thoughts, he said, "This is a small town, Kelly. Doctors and pharmacies talk frequently. You will not find anyone else in town who will write you the prescription you want."

With that, Kelly's eyes filled with tears, which then slowly and consistently fell down her cheeks. "What am I going to do?" she whispered.

"I will tell you exactly what to expect and give you tips on how to manage your pain. Would you like to call your dad so he can hear this information as well?"

"No. Just tell me what to do. I will tell him," she lied.

"Okay. Well, first of all, the process could take anywhere from five to ten days. Percocet stays in your system for a few days. So, your withdrawal symptoms will begin when your body expects the next dose, and you don't oblige. As the withdrawal process begins, you will feel like you are experiencing a cold or flu and a stomach bug all at the same time. There are other symptoms which may occur. Some of these include anxiety, cold flashes, depression, increased heart rate, insomnia, irritation, tingling in your arms and legs, and of course, the nausea and vomiting," he paused to let her process the information. "Are you sure you don't want to call your dad?"

"I'm sure," she managed to reply.

He nodded grimly and then continued, "The intense and uncomfortable symptoms usually resolve within the first week. And most symptoms should even out and be gone within about 4-5 weeks. There is a slim chance you could develop protracted withdrawal symptoms which can last months after you have stopped taking Percocet. But that is a rare occurrence and I don't expect that to happen with you."

"Four to five weeks?" Kelly asks incredulously. "I will feel like I have the flu for four to five weeks? Plus my leg will hurt?" She covered her face with her hands and cried even more.

"After the first few days, it won't be so bad. Kelly, you can do this. What's more, you must do this. I will give you my home phone number in case you need me."

"You will?" she asked.

"Yes, I will. I have known your mom and dad for years, and I have great respect for both of them."

"Are you going to tell them?"

"No, I won't tell them. But I firmly believe that you should tell them. They could help you."

Kelly nodded, but had no intention of telling her parents. They had too much to handle already. They didn't need drug addiction to add to their list of woes.

When Kelly returned to the waiting room, Jill knew she had been crying.

"Are you okay?" she whispered with great concern.

"Yeah. I will be," Kelly replied with trembling voice.

Later that night, Kelly made sure the door to her bedroom was closed before she picked up the phone extension to place a call. After several rings, a familiar voice answered.

"Chris, this is Kelly. What are you doing for Spring Break?"

And so it was, her faithful friend Chris, helped her through the first days of withdrawal, two hours away from her family. If she was lucky, her parents would never know.

CHAPTER

"Well, I guess I'll see you at Orientation."

"Yeah, I'm looking forward to it. Are you all ready?"

"I think so. It's weird, though, you know? This hasn't been the best year, but I made it. Thanks for all your help, Chris. You know I couldn't have made it through that week without you. You've seen me at my worst, for sure. I'm glad we are still friends in spite everything."

"I'll always be your friend, Kelly."

"I know that. Especially now. I hope we can see each other a lot at State," she said hesitantly. She didn't want Chris to get the wrong idea. She did like him, but she couldn't decide if they were just good friends, or heading down the road to more. And she didn't know which way she wanted things to go. Time would tell. They ended the conversation with promises to check in with each other during Orientation, which was still a week away.

Kelly placed the phone back on the hook, and then stretched out on her bed after she scooted piles of clothes to the other side. She glanced around her childhood bedroom, seeing those things so familiar with a different eye. Life was about to change, and she knew that it would never be the same. In many ways she was relieved. She had wanted to get away for so long, to run away from the difficulties all around her. But this life was all she knew. It was hard, but predictable. She was needed here. And being needed was a blessing and a curse. She liked to be needed, and yet felt overwhelmed by it at the same time.

Tired of such deep thoughts, she glanced once again at the shelves, which lined the far wall. Childish storybooks shared the space with high school textbooks. Leaning prominently in front was her high school diploma, still framed in it's leather-ish folder. She had made it—not just through the academic requirements, but through so much more ... the stresses of home, the pain of her recovery, the agony of withdrawing from addiction. Surely, things would change for the better now. Surely, she had paid her dues through the challenges of life. *Surely, right?* she thought, as she fought the feeling of impending doom. She couldn't remember many days that were "footloose and fancy-free" as her grandmother often said. Not since she was six years old. *Yes, surely the coming years will be better.* She was determined to believe it to be true.

Kelly carried another load up the stairs to her dorm room. She had been assigned to room 210 in Hightower Dormitory. Her leg was already feeling sore, and they weren't halfway finished unloading. It was going to be a long day. Will had come with Kelly to help her move in, and the two of them had worked long and hard packing and loading, now unloading and unpacking. Her thoughts traveled back to the early hours of the morning, as she said goodbye to her mother. There was pain in her eyes, though Sadie tried to hide it. *I think mom wanted to be here today even more than I wanted her to be,* Kelly thought as she climbed the stairs. She had seen all the mothers and daughters laughing, unpacking, and hanging curtains together. She had seen the tearful, good-bye hugs and she wished once again her story had a different storyline. *It is what it is,* Kelly thought, abruptly ending her train of thought. She had stopped at the landing to catch her breath, and suddenly heard a voice behind her.

"Need help?"

Chris. How did he always show up just at the right time? She let out a loud sigh and replied, "I sure do! Perfect timing!" And she turned to hand him her heavy load, thankful for a true friend.

"A friend in need is a friend indeed. That's what my dad always says."

"Yeah, I think Benjamin Franklin said it first, though," he replied with a grin.

"I don't care who said it. It's true. And thanks, by the way."

He just smiled in response, and together they headed up the stairs.

Life in college provided freedom which Kelly loved. She could do what she wanted, when she wanted, and with whomever she wanted. Her affinity for vodka and Dr. Pepper expanded to many other concoctions. And on occasion, she went even a step further and tried whatever was offered for an additional high. She was finally able to put her troubled past behind her—at least while she was in the midst of the party. In the midst of the party she could forget. The problem was, when the party was over, she well remembered her issues, and coupled with the guilt of her behavior, she felt even worse.

On one such night, she found herself partying with friends, including Chris. The next morning, to her horror, she realized she had not just forgotten her problems, she had also forgotten her morals, her honor, and the one boundary she had managed to maintain. She had crossed the line with Chris, and she knew their friendship would never be the same. He, too, seemed awkward and ashamed, and she knew without asking he, too, wished they had been aware enough to say no.

The following weeks, they both found themselves avoiding each other. When Kelly saw him on campus, she walked in a different direction. She felt sure he was doing the same thing.

One day right before Spring Break, she came face to face with Chris and their inevitable conversation could not be avoided. They found themselves in the stairwell of the Lee Hall on campus. He was going up, she down and they both arrived at the landing at the same time. They both smiled a timid, surprised smile, and Chris was first to break the silence.

"Kelly, I've been wanting to talk to you for a long time now," he began.

"Yeah. Me, too," she replied.

"Well, I guess we both could admit we made a mistake," he continued awkwardly. "But I really do miss spending time with you. Do you think we could put that behind us and go back to the way it was before?"

"Yeah. I would like that. I'm really sorry about everything, including avoiding you for the past few weeks," she offered.

"I'm sorry, too. I really am. I don't want to do anything to hurt our friendship," he replied.

"Me, neither. Let's just put that behind us and move on, okay?" she said with a smile.

"Agreed," he said as he flashed her a sincere smile. They parted ways thinking all was well and settled. Little did they know the repercussions of that fateful night still remained to be seen.

CHAPTER

11

Kelly lay on her bed in her dorm room and moaned. *What is wrong with me?* she said out loud, though no one was there to answer. She was glad her roommate had left the room early. She was tired of faking it. For days now, she had felt terrible. Dizzy, nauseous, and so very tired. She felt a bit like she had a hangover, but she knew that couldn't be it. Ever since that night with Chris, she had cut way back on the partying. She did not want to repeat that mistake ever again. She forced herself to get up and made her way down the hallway to the common bathroom. *Maybe I will feel better after I shower,* she thought, hoping it would be true.

She showered, dried off and started back down the hall, when a wave of nausea hit, sending her racing back to the bathroom. She felt a bit better in the moments after she lost the remainder of her undigested dinner, but only a bit.

She wanted to skip class, and this time it would be legit. But she had already taken all five of the allowed absences and she couldn't risk a bad grade. She knew her parents had sacrificed to send her to school without school loans, and she didn't want to disappoint them. As she dressed, she wondered once again what could be the source of her illness. And then a thought hit her so forcefully she moaned out loud. *Please, God. Don't let it be that,* she thought. *The Percocet. Dr. Roberts said in rare cases the withdrawal symptoms could last for months. Is it possible they have returned?* She dressed as quickly as possible, frantic thoughts racing through her mind. She was determined to find the one person who knew what she had been through when she had gone through the Percocet withdrawal. Chris. *I need to talk to Chris,* she thought as she hurried out the door.

After an hour of searching in all the places she thought Chris might be—the cafeteria, the Student Union, and Duggar Dorm—she finally found him in the stacks in the library, studying for a test.

"Chris," she whispered with urgency.

"Hey! What are you doing here?" he whispered back.

"I need to talk to you. You are the only person I can talk to about this. Can you take a break?" she asked.

"Sure. I would love an excuse to take a break," he answered in his typical good-natured way.

They walked side by side in silence until they exited the library. He pointed to a bench under a tree and they did not speak until both were seated.

"Okay, what's up?" he began.

"I haven't been feeling very well. Dizzy, sick to my stomach. I even threw up this morning. It brought back all those terrible memories of last Spring Break. Do you think I could still be having withdrawal symptoms? The doctor said in rare cases the withdrawal symptoms could last for months." she asked, panic rising as she spoke.

"He said months, and it's been over a year. Do you really

think that could be it?" he asked calmly.

"I don't know. I guess I panicked."

"Also, he said it could last for months. Did he also say symptoms could stop and then start back again months later?"

"No. You're right. Gosh," she took a deep breath. "Thanks, Chris. I guess I just panicked. It's probably something I ate, or a virus, or something like that," she said rising from the bench.

"I will let you get back to studying. Thanks so much. I will see you later." She flashed a sincere smile, which he returned, and they walked away in different directions.

A week later, Kelly found herself once again in the doctor's office. This clinic was only a couple of miles from campus and they advertised themselves as a "walk-in" clinic with short wait times. *Sounds good to me,* Kelly thought as she pulled into the only available parking space. Two hours later, she finally sat in the exam room waiting on the doctor. He entered a short while later, and introduced himself as Dr. Cain. His calm nature and clear, green eyes put Kelly instantly at ease. She described her symptoms, which had continued throughout the week. And she sheepishly told him of her former addiction to Percocet. She saw no judgment from him, just pure professionalism, which made Kelly feel even more comfortable.

"I don't think your past experiences with Percocet would cause your symptoms at this point—unless you have used Percocet again recently?"

"No, sir. I haven't had one in over a year," she said with conviction.

"Well, then, let's do a little blood work and see if anything shows up. We will test for common things like mono or strep. Sometimes those infections can cause nausea and vomiting, as well as overall fatigue. We also need to do a pregnancy test just to be sure," he glanced up at Kelly for an affirmative at that last statement.

Kelly felt her face grow hot and red, but nodded yes. Her heart began to pound with the thought of pregnancy. *Surely, not,* she tried to convince herself.

Ten minutes later, the doctor re-entered the room and gave her the news. Positive pregnancy test. Panic set in immediately as the reality of those words came at her from every direction. She felt as if she had been caught up in a strong undertow, taking her further and further from the safe shore.

"Oh, no. Please, no. Can you check again? Are you sure?" The nurse stepped forward to calmly take her hand, just as the tears began to flow. The doctor spoke encouraging words, but she heard none of it. She felt as if she were drowning. The last words she heard as she left the exam room included "options" and "your choice" and "Memphis clinics". She wandered to her car in a daze, and before she could drive away, she was hit once again by a wave of nausea. *What am I going to do?* she thought after she lost her lunch in the parking lot.

Kelly drove for two hours all around Starkville, with no particular destination in mind. She drove past Oby's, her favorite restaurant, and then through the Cotton District where she saw a couple of her friends' cars parked. She didn't stop. She couldn't stop. She didn't want to see anyone. She didn't want to tell anyone. She couldn't imagine what this news would do to her parents. *What am I going to do?* she thought over and over, with no answers surfacing despite her continued questioning. At the end of the second hour of her random cruising, only one thing surfaced with clarity. She needed to find Chris. He deserved to know. And besides, he was her go-to in times of trouble. She knew she could trust him.

Though she knew she looked terrible, she didn't care. She went to his dorm, and then the library. Still no Chris. She looked in the Student Union and in the cafeteria, and then finally found him off campus sitting with two pretty freshmen girls at The Grill. She walked straight up to their table, suddenly very aware of her unkempt appearance.

She ignored the girls and looked straight at Chris. "I need to talk to you," she said.

Both girls looked at each other with raised eyebrows, then looked down at the table with slight smiles on their faces. She ignored them and said once again, "I really need to talk to you. It can't wait."

"Sure. No problem," he said, and then turning his attention to his companions, he said, "See you girls later," and cast a cheerful smile their way.

They walked in silence until they reached a private booth away from the crowd of people.

"Okay, shoot. What's up?" he said, slightly irritated.

"I just came from the doctor's office," she began, looking at the ground.

"I'm pregnant," she said flatly, as she glanced up to see his reaction.

Chris's face went pale, and his mouth fell open, yet no words formed.

"Are you sure?" he asked, his own panic rising.

"Yes, I'm sure. They did a blood test." Neither said a word for several seconds until Kelly continued, "What are we going to do?" she said, her own panic surpassing his.

"Are you sure I'm the father?" he said coldly, watching her face to see her reaction.

"Chris! Are you serious? Is that what you think of me? Of course, you are the father!" she whispered roughly, shocked at his accusation. And then she began to sob loudly, both hands covering her face.

She felt his hand on her back, and when he spoke, his words were softer, kinder. "I'm sorry, Kelly. I know you're not like that. I'm just in shock. What are you going to do?"

"I don't know. I don't have a clue. But I do know this—I can never tell my parents. Not ever. This would kill them," she said with conviction.

They sat for many minutes in silence, staring straight ahead, seeing nothing but all the different scenarios playing through their minds' eyes. And none of those scenarios brought relief. After a while, Kelly sat up straighter, determination growing deep within her. And she began to repeat the last words she heard from the doctor, which included "options" and "my choice" and "Memphis clinics".

CHAPTER

12

The day was overcast and gray, unseasonably cold for the middle of May. Kelly and Chris drove below the speed limit all the way down Highway 78. They were anxious to get it over with, and yet something unseen held them back. They tried hard not to think—or speak—of what they were about to do. Since this was the only thing on their minds, they simply chose not to speak at all. They exited onto Perkins Avenue and drove until they reached Poplar Avenue and made a left toward downtown. Still, the only time they spoke was when Chris, who was driving, asked for clarification from the map Kelly held in her lap. They arrived twenty minutes before the scheduled appointment, parked in the closest parking spot, and sat in silence for a few minutes before gathering the courage to open the door.

Chris reached into the pocket of his jeans and took out a wad of cash. He handed it to Kelly and said, "I'm sorry I couldn't come up with all of it."

Kelly put the cash in her purse and replied, "It's okay. I understand. I didn't have any money either, so my friend, Jill, let me borrow $200. I'm going to pay her back."

"Did you tell her what it is for?" he asked nervously.

"Yes, but don't worry. I didn't mention your name. I trust her. She won't tell anyone," she answered defensively.

As soon as they got out of the car, they saw ten to twelve people with signs gathered on the sidewalk in front of the clinic. Their faces were serious, etched in anger. Their signs were words of hatred and disdain announcing the sin and shame of those who dared to enter the clinic. Kelly and Chris shot each other a look of dread, anticipating what was about to happen. And sure enough, as they approached the doors of the clinic the bearers of the signs shouted aloud the written words. And these words were aimed directly at Chris and Kelly.

"Stop! Don't do it!"

"It's murder!"

"You will go to hell!"

"It's a baby, not a blob!"

They picked up the pace toward the doors and were practically running when they finally opened them and ran inside to the safety of the waiting room. They looked around them and saw several people waiting, mostly in pairs. Some were obviously couples, others looked as if they were mothers and daughters. They all glanced in the direction of the doors as they opened, but quickly lowered their gaze to the floor. No one seemed interested in conversation or even eye contact. The heaviness of the room took Kelly's breath away. She thought for a split second about leaving, but knew she would have to face the sidewalk crowd if she left. *Besides, I have made up my mind. This is my only choice and I can't back out now*, she thought with determination.

They both sat in uncomfortable silence looking at the floor, until Kelly's name was called. Slowly, she rose from her seat and looked at Chris.

"It's going to be okay. You can do this," he whispered tenderly.

Kelly nodded in reply and walked toward the wooden door where the nurse was waiting. She was almost to the door when Chris called her back for a moment. He rose from his seat and met her half way across the room.

"Hey, I'm going to ride around for a while. I will be back in just a little bit."

When Kelly gave him a confused look, he answered her unspoken question. "Look, I feel really uncomfortable in here. I will be back before you are done, I promise. I just need some air."

She nodded her understanding. If only she could leave for a while. But she couldn't. She had no choice.

"Want me to keep up with your purse?" he said as he pointed to the bag on her shoulder.

"Yeah, thanks," she said as she handed over the bag.

He quickly walked out the front doors and she continued toward the waiting nurse and the unknown experience behind the wooden door.

The nurse led Kelly down a narrow hallway until they turned left into a small office. She pointed to the chair in front of the desk, and Kelly sat down silently. The nurse sat at the desk and began asking her questions.

"How far along are you?"

"Do you have any pre-existing medical conditions?"

"Sign here, here, and here."

"And now, we will need the complete payment before you start. Four hundred."

Kelly froze for just a moment, and her heart raced even more. "I'm sorry, but my …. Well, uh. He took my purse. Can I pay after? He said he will be back before I'm done."

The nurse suddenly turned cold and even more distant. "No, we cannot do the procedure until you have paid in full."

"I promise, he will be right back."

The nurse rather roughly gathered the paperwork and placed a paper clip over the stack. She then got up and motioned for Kelly to follow her. As they got near to the wooden door once again, the nurse curtly said, "You can stay in the waiting room until he returns. *If* he returns. But I will warn you, if he is not back in the next forty-five minutes, it will be too late to start the procedure today and you will have to make another appointment. You also should know that if your calculations are correct, you are getting very close to the legal cut-off. Another week and we will be unable to do the procedure." She abruptly closed the door and left Kelly standing just inside the waiting room. Once again, all eyes in the room quickly looked at Kelly, then back down to the floor. She walked to the far side of the room, choosing a chair which faced the doors, so she could see Chris the moment he returned. Her heart pounded and with every minute which passed, her anger toward Chris grew.

I can't believe he left me here.
Where the heck is he?
When is he getting back?
I wish he would hurry up.
If he doesn't hurry, I won't be able to do it at all.

I can't have the baby. I can't do that to my parents. They will hate me.

Maybe this is a way out.

The last thought caught her off guard. Somewhere in the back of her mind she remembered learning that God provides a way out of sin. Her parents had always made sure she had attended church each week. Words from her past came clearly to her mind. She could not have recalled them if she had been asked to, however, now, unbidden, they came clearly—almost as if someone had spoken them aloud to her.

No temptation has overtaken you except what is common to mankind. And God is faithful; he will not let you be tempted beyond what you can bear. But when you are tempted, he will also provide a way out so that you can endure it.

The thought nearly took her breath away. *I could just walk away,* she thought. But then she felt a coldness overtake her heart. She pushed the weakness down—down, down into the deep places of her soul, and suddenly she felt hard and cold and even more determined. Five minutes later, Chris walked through the door, her purse hanging awkwardly from his right hand. She walked up to him and glared.

"I need my purse to pay," she hissed. "Don't leave again."

He simply nodded and handed her the purse. She walked through the wooden door, not waiting to be called back.

Chris supported Kelly with one hand and awkwardly tried to open the door to the hotel room with the other. They had a hard time finding a room in Memphis, as the annual Memphis in May event had brought in thousands of guests. After a few moments of struggle, he opened the door wide and let her in, all the while still holding onto her arm. He made sure she was safely on the bed before he let go. He placed her purse and overnight bag on the floor, and laid down on the other bed. For a while, they both simply stared at the ceiling. Then, Chris turned to her and said, "Are you okay?"

"Yeah," she stated simply and directly.

"Do you want to talk about it?" he asked hesitantly.

"No. Not ever. I don't ever want to talk about it," she said flatly. And with that, she turned to the side, away from Chris, and pulled her knees up to her chest—into a fetal position, much like her baby had been only hours before. She lay there perfectly still and tried to think of anything except the experience she had just endured. She could hear the rain pouring down outside. *April showers bring May flowers,* she thought randomly. *But it is already May. The flowers haven't come. The storms remain.* This was her last thought before she fell asleep, blocking out the rain and the memories, until she met both in the horror of her dreams.

She awoke with a start, heart pounding, and sweat pouring down the sides of her face. She looked at Chris who slept soundly in the opposite bed. For a few moments, she could not discern what was a dream and what was reality. Unwanted memories flooded through her mind in no particular order and she could not will them away even though she tried. The sound of the machine, loud and constant, still echoed in her mind. And they had said it wouldn't hurt. But it did hurt, so badly she could barely stand it. Just at the point she was about to yell for the doctor to stop, the machine went silent and it was over. Though the doctor was as cold and sterile as the room, the words of the nurse were sickeningly sweet.

"You are doing great."

"Hang in there. It's almost over."

"You did so well. I'm proud of you."

How could she be proud of me, Kelly thought bitterly. This same nurse had briefed her before the procedure with encouraging words and a video which explained the procedure as if it was as simple as a tooth extraction.

"You are doing the right thing, Honey. You are too young for this responsibility. You have your whole life ahead of you."

"That's what I keep telling myself," Kelly replied. "And I know my baby will go to Heaven," she added without thinking.

"Oh, Honey. You can't think like that. You will never go through with it if you do. No, the fact is this is not a baby. It is a mass of tissue that needs to be removed. It's just like a little butterbean, Honey."

A butterbean? Kelly thought incredulously. But she kept silent and tried to think of a butterbean as the machine droned on and on and the pain grew greater and greater.

After the procedure the nurse took her into a different kind of waiting room. This room was filled with girls, many who looked to be around her age. The room was not silent like the front room. This room was polluted with sobs and moans and groans and hysterical weeping. Kelly sat in a faux leather medical recliner and tried to drown out the noise with sheer concentration. Something deep inside her seemed to crack. She suddenly felt cold, lifeless, and detached from what was taking place around her. She was the only dry-eyed girl in the room. The nurse returned and complimented her on how well she was doing, how proud she was of her. Kelly just nodded at her, but couldn't think of a word of response. After a while, the nurse returned.

"Honey, you are doing so well! I think you are ready to go. Do you have someone waiting for you in the waiting room?"

"Yes. Chris," Kelly replied.

"Well, I will get Chris to pull the car to the back entrance. That way you don't have to walk past those unpleasant people at the front. I will be right back."

Kelly just stared at her as she left the room, feeling detached from this surreal experience.

Thunder outside roused Kelly from her memories, and she gingerly sat up on the bed to watch the rain through the window, glad that Chris had failed to draw the curtains. She wished she could go out in the storm and let the rain wash away the memories, wash away the stain she felt she would always have. Instead, she simply watched and listened to the rain until it lulled her back to sleep, though a peaceful sleep she would not find for many days.

CHAPTER

13

At the same time, across town a woman named Tammy screamed out in pain as the contractions came in rapid succession. *It's not supposed to be like this,* she thought. *It's too soon. I thought I was only 35 weeks. But then, I don't really know. It was just a guess.* She concentrated on breathing as the nurse had instructed her to do, letting the air out slowly between her teeth two times, and then a big blow until all of the air was out of her lungs. Breathe in a deep breath and start over again. Over and over and over. Time disappeared and succumbed to merely anticipating when the next pain would begin, rise, and decline. The time in between contractions was spent dreading what was to come, and dwelling on random thoughts which ran through her mind in no particular order.

She thought about how her day had begun. She would have never gotten in that truck if she had known she would go into labor. They had just pestered her so much that she had finally given up—just like she always did. Roy and Silvia seemed to dictate her whole life. She lived on their property in the old trailer just down from their house. She was not living in the lap of luxury, that's for sure. But the price was right and they were pretty nice—at least as long as she did everything they asked. Sometimes they asked a lot. But she had lost her conscience years ago, and now all that remained was keeping them happy so she had a place to live. She knew deep down it was more than a place to live, but she didn't have the energy to decipher why they had such a controlling hold over her. Just like today, she usually just did what they said to do.

They had talked her into going by shaming her. They poked fun at the fact she had never experienced Memphis in May, as if they were expert travelers. She had heard about it and had even read up on it when they started pestering her. She thought if she sounded smart about it, maybe they wouldn't make fun of her. She had spouted off all she knew about the festival, hoping they would take her seriously for once. She told them how it started back when she was a teenager in 1977, and how each year the event focused on a different country as a theme. This year, 1992, the salute was to Italy. Ambassadors, performance groups, and exhibits were scheduled to come throughout the month of May. She had always loved the idea of Italy and used to daydream about going there one day. She didn't think about that much anymore. In fact, she didn't think about any of her old dreams and desires. She just existed in a tiny world of a trailer, a small wooden house, and a couple who controlled her. That world was about to change and that was one of the reasons Roy was so mean to her now.

Roy started out like a big brother to her. She was very close to Silvia, and Roy came with her. He would help her out when she needed it, was kind and friendly, and seemed content to let her live on their property almost as if she were family. But then came the strings attached. And there were many. She agreed to help him with his "errands" even when it became clear that if caught, she would land in jail, or worse yet, find herself in a deal gone bad. She pretty much did whatever Roy and Silvia told her to do, with two exceptions: 1) She refused to abort her baby when she found out she was pregnant, and 2) She refused Roy's advances when his friendliness turned wicked. For those reasons alone, Roy had turned on her, and his wrath could be dangerous. Now, she simply tried to stay out of his way.

The ride to Memphis was fairly miserable, given her condition and the fact that the air conditioner broke. At least there was a cool, though noisy breeze with the windows down. They had parked near the Orpheum and had walked down to Tom Lee Park on the riverbank, dodging the crowd and trying to scout out the best spot. Today was the day of the Sunset Symphony, which wrapped up the Memphis in May events. The edge of the Mississippi River was packed with people crammed like sardines, trying to make room for their blankets and lawn chairs. She was surprised at the crowd, especially given the overcast skies and threatening forecast. However, she had chosen to come, just like the rest of them, so maybe she was just as crazy. *It wasn't really my choice,* she thought, but decided not to dwell on that fact. She was relieved when they finally found a spot to settle. Her legs were swollen and her back hurt something awful. All she wanted was to sit in her old yellow lawn chair and rest. She pushed the crisscross yellow mesh seat forward by grasping the faded aluminum frame and settled in beside Silvia. Roy sat on the other side of Silvia as the final bookend. Silvia was the glue between them so her spot in the middle—separating the other two— seemed appropriate. She put her bag in front of her chair and propped her feet on it, in an effort to ease the swelling. She had not been sitting very long when her head fell to her chest and she dozed off, despite the crowd, noise, and loud music.

"Hey there, pretty lady!" a male voice slurred.

"I said, hey there!" he repeated, determined to get her attention.

She opened her eyes, quite dazed and confused. She looked over at Silva and Roy, who giggled and sneered, respectively.

She looked toward the man who had so rudely interrupted her nap. What she saw—and smelled—reminded her of a trail of others with whom she had associated. Indignation rose up within her.

"Excuse me?" she said coolly.

"I said, hey there!" he answered.

"Hello," she answered, but kept her eyes straight ahead.

"What's your name?" he persisted.

"I'm not sure that is any of your business." She was irritated to be awakened, and irritated at what he represented in her life. *What is he doing*, she thought angrily. *Can't he see I'm eight months pregnant?*

"My name is Tammy Thomas. And if you don't want to fist fight a pregnant woman, you better just leave."

He looked at her stomach, obviously too drunk to have noticed the protruding belly before. "Oh, sorry, Ms. Tammy. I didn't mean any harm." He tipped his baseball cap and staggered to the next group of females just ahead of them.

Tammy fumed long after he left. It only added fuel to the fire when Silvia called him her boyfriend, and Roy glared at her as if she had invited the attention. She decided to walk around, desperately needing a break from her traveling companions. She stood up and winced. Her lower back ached and the pain traveled to her side. Her stomach grew tight and then lessened a bit, as she continued to walk closer to the river.

The sky seemed to grow darker and darker with every step. She paused for a moment to rub her lower back with her right hand and looked up at the dark clouds which were starting to churn. *Oh, great. It's gonna storm while we are all out here in the open. That's just great*, she fumed.

She stood for just a moment and listened to the music playing. Suddenly, the sky opened up and sent a flood drenching her and everyone around her. She hurried back to Roy and Silvia, who had gathered up the chairs and bags and were ready to leave. Together, the three walked as quickly as they could, given the crowd as well as Tammy's condition. They were almost to the truck when her drenched body experienced another flood—warm liquid followed by excruciating pain. She cried out and her companions turned to see what the problem was.

"My water broke," she said through clenched teeth. Silvia rushed to help her as Roy remained planted, obviously irritated at the turn of events.

Back in the present, a kind nurse wiped her brow and soothed her with encouraging words.

"You're doing great, Tammy."

"It is almost time to push."

"You can do this."

Yes, I can, Tammy thought. *I can do this. I will do this. No one can take my baby away from me, not even Roy. This is my second chance to make something of my life, to do something good for a change.* She felt empowered for the first time in a very long while.

Forty-five minutes later, the doctor spoke calmly but with authority. "Okay, Tammy. We need one more push. Bear down hard."

Tammy pushed with all her might, letting out a scream in the process. Seconds later she felt a warm swoosh, and then a tiny cry picked up where hers left off. A beautiful feeling of peace settled around her and tears of happiness unlike she had ever experienced fell gracefully. Her second chance had arrived at last.

CHAPTER

14

Chris reluctantly opened the door to the "party room" of the frat house. He pushed sideways through the crowd, trying not to knock the contents of the red plastic cups most of the attendees held in their hands. He had no problem with their choices, he just didn't feel up to it himself. In fact, he didn't feel up to much of anything these days. Ever since he and Kelly had returned from Memphis, he had simply existed in a world of lethargy. He couldn't concentrate for very long and he knew if something didn't change quickly, his grades were going to suffer. He had begun to hide away in the "stacks" of the library, hoping for a quiet place he could actually think again—or rather, think of the content of his textbooks rather than the experience of that fateful trip to Memphis. Though he wouldn't have ever admitted it, he had also chosen the "stacks" as his new home away from home, because there he could hide away from everyone else in his life—especially Kelly. He knew he should try to talk to her, but he just couldn't do it. And truth be told, he knew she didn't want to see him either. He felt certain that this time, their experience together had forever changed their friendship. They couldn't just decide to go back to the way it was before. They could never go back now. So, he hid in the stacks away from Kelly, away from his friends, away from reality.

The only reason he had come to this party was to appease his roommate who had incessantly pestered him about attending.

"What's wrong with you, Man?"

"You aren't acting yourself. You used to be the life of the party. What's happened to you?"

"I expect to see you at the party tonight," he had said before he left the room. Chris realized then that he must make an appearance just to shut the guy up. And so, he now pushed through the crowd toward a far corner where he could listen to the band and stay long enough to prove to his roommate that he was okay.

But am I okay? he thought to himself. He didn't like to admit it, but he felt himself sinking to a very dark place. *I better talk to someone before I go crazy,* he thought, but quickly dispelled the notion. *Nope. I am going to my grave with this one*, he concluded.

From his spot in the corner, he could see a rowdy group of people push their way to the front of the dance floor, as the band began the first chords of the Rolling Stones song, "Satisfaction". Cups in hand, the group danced as one, singing at the top of their lungs, at least during the chorus.

> *I can't get no satisfaction*
> *I can't get no satisfaction*
> *'Cause I try and I try and I try and I try*
> *I can't get no, I can't get no*

Chris could feel the vibration of the bass and though he used to be the center of it all, he felt detached from the party, the music, and the crowd of people. He looked closer at the rowdy group and saw Kelly in the middle of them. Singing loud and free, holding cup high in the air, she looked on the outside like she was having the time of her life. That is, until she saw him in the corner. She stopped right in the middle of the song and stared at him, her drunken state of happiness, suddenly serious and stunned. It was as if the sight of him simply paralyzed her. It only lasted a moment. She seemed to snap out of it quickly and went back to the hysteria of the crowded dance floor. But Chris had seen enough to know—she was spinning out of control.

Ten days later, Chris found himself knocking on the office door of David Willis, the area director of Campus Crusade for Christ. David was thirty-five and showed the beginning signs of middle age. He was graying at his temples and had begun wearing his shirt untucked, which though it appeared up-to-date, also conveniently hid the extra fifteen pounds he had acquired in the past few years. His deep blue eyes were framed with "smile lines," which on the rare occasion he noticed them made him smile even more because to him they represented a happy life. It was the warmth and sincerity of those eyes that made even acquaintances feel as if they had a good friend. He had worked with Campus Crusade his entire adult life and felt honored to minister to students in the same way he had once experienced.

Campus Crusade was founded in 1951 at the University of California by Bill Bright as an interdenominational evangelical Christian organization for university students. Chris didn't know anything about it—all he knew was some of the guys he respected the most participated in their programs.

"Come on in," a male voice said from the other side of the door. He entered a bright room, simply furnished. Immediately, he noticed the framed photos covering the walls—mostly college-aged students, but some photos of children from foreign lands mixed in.

As he entered, a tall coed with dark hair rose from the chair opposite the desk, where the middle-aged man, obviously the director, sat.

"Oh, sorry to interrupt," Chris said, slightly embarrassed.

"Not at all," the student answered as he held out his hand in greeting. The two shook hands as the student introduced himself. "I'm Stan. Stan Williams."

"Hey. I'm Chris Smith. Nice to meet you," replied Chris. "I can come back later."

"No problem, I was just leaving." He turned to David and said, "Hey, Man, thanks for the study materials. I'll see you at Cru." And then turning back to Chris, Stan said, "Chris, nice to meet you. Hope to see you at Cru sometime. We meet Tuesdays at 8:00 in Lee Hall Auditorium."

"Oh, well. Yeah, maybe," Chris replied awkwardly.

When Stan left the office, David invited Chris to sit in the chair Stan had just vacated. "What can I help you with, Chris," David began. His friendly and laid back manner immediately put Chris at ease.

Five minutes later, Chris had opened up much more than he had planned.

"So, you are simply worried about this friend of yours, the one who had the abortion?"

Chris looked down at his hands, suddenly unable to look

David in the eyes. "Yeah, that's right."

"Well, Chris, you are right to be concerned. It does sound like she is spiraling out of control. But it's understandable. Statistics say that women who have had an abortion have over 80% greater chance for mental health issues like depression and anxiety than women who have not had an abortion. They even have a 150% greater chance of suicide. They don't tell you that in the clinic when you are making the decision, but it's true. So many women have an abortion so they can get rid of the problem, only to discover they have invited more problems than they could have ever imagined. And that is just the statistics for the women. The men involved in an abortion can have big problems, too." He paused for just a moment when he saw a change in Chris's face as he heard the last sentence. But Chris didn't say a word, and when the silence became awkward, David continued.

"You know, Chris, I have so many people sit just where you are right now and tell me heartbreaking stories—stories they never thought they would share with anyone. But they are looking for hope and I have that to offer them," he paused again, but Chris said nothing.

"Sometimes, when someone sits in that chair and they are concerned for a friend … Well, sometimes they are more involved in the situation than they want to admit. And they need hope, too." He looked straight at Chris and saw tears fill his eyes though he willed them away quickly. Chris knew that he knew. There was no need for pretense.

"Will God forgive me?" Chris said simply. Though dry-eyed now, his face took on a look of desperation.

"Yes, Chris. God will forgive you. I am certain of that. But you have to ask Him."

"How do I do that?" Chris asked, desperation giving way to hope.

"Well, it's quite simple. I can help you. Really, I am the perfect one to help you—because, Chris, about twenty years ago, I was you. I was in a seat very similar to that one, looking for help and hope. My girlfriend and I thought an abortion would make the problem go away, but it didn't. Not by a long shot. It is a hard process. It is something that creeps up on you at odd times—even after all these years. But when that happens, I have to preach the gospel to myself all over again. The gospel is simply this: Christ came to save us sinners. He took it on Himself, so we wouldn't have to bear it anymore. And He can take it away as far as the east is from the west—that's what the Bible says. Do you want to pray, Chris?"

"Yeah, I do—more than anything," he replied. And in that moment, hope was born and healing began.

CHAPTER  15

Tammy popped the top to the bottle of formula. She only had two cans of the pre-made kind; the rest was powder. She saved the pre-made kind for emergencies and this was an emergency, she reasoned. It was two in the morning and Tessa had been screaming for two hours. Non-stop. Tammy had rocked her and walked her and changed her and even let her scream for a while in her bed. During that time, she had gone outside and sat on the wooden steps of the trailer. When she still heard the incessant cries, she covered her ears and cried. She didn't know what to do.

This is so much harder than I thought. Why didn't she come with an instruction manual? Am I just supposed to know what to do instinctively? Some kind of mothering gene or something? If that's it, then I am missing the gene, she thought miserably.

She poured the white liquid into the bottle and heated it in the tiny microwave sitting on the counter. She shook it up and then tested it on the inside of her wrist like she had seen in a movie a long time ago. It burned her arm. *Must have been too long in the microwave*, she thought. Tears of frustration sprang to her eyes once again. *Seems all I ever do is cry*, she thought, which brought on more tears which ran down her face as she cooled the bottle in the cold water from the kitchen faucet.

She went to the crib and picked up Tessa and for the first time since the birth, Tammy felt angry at her baby. So angry it scared her. She put Tessa back down as they both continued to cry. Tammy walked to the cabinet above the sink and pulled out the glass bottle. She grabbed a dirty plastic cup and poured the amber colored drink. It didn't stay in the cup for long as Tammy guzzled the glassful as she was standing by the sink. She poured more into the cup and sat on the steps outside once again. The weather was hot and sticky, a typical Mississippi night. As she sipped the second cup of Jack Daniels, she felt the warm burn give way to a calm she desperately needed. She concentrated on the sound of the locusts, which were in abundance in the woods surrounding her trailer. The music of the locusts was almost loud enough to drown out the screams coming from inside the trailer. Almost. Calmer, Tammy rose once again and went inside. She grabbed the bottle from the counter, now thoroughly cooled and headed toward the crib once again.

Tessa latched onto the bottle and gulped with surprising force. *She's a strong one*, Tammy thought. *And it's a good thing. She's gonna have to be strong living in this world.* And with glazed eyes, Tammy laid down on the bed, Tessa still in her arms. And the two fell sound asleep side by side.

Two hours away, Kelly also indulged in the same amber liquid and she, too, sat outside listening to the sound of the locusts. She, too, was trying to drown out a sound, which never seemed to stop. The sound of the machine, which took away her child. No matter how much she tried to tell herself it was just a mass of tissue, she could never see it that way. And so, she drank. And she smoked and popped pills and tried to find comfort in the arms of those who could never really give her what she needed.

The next day, Kelly dragged herself out of the twin bed in her dorm room and stepped over piles of clothes scattered all over the floor. She walked down the hallway to the bathroom and splashed water on her face. She had overslept again and didn't have time for a shower, so she brushed her teeth and combed her fingers through her hair before pulling it back up in a ponytail. She paused just a moment and stared at herself in the mirror. She could hardly recognize herself. She had lost weight, and her cheeks were pail and sunken. She pinched them just a bit rather than take time for makeup. Her eyes had bags and dark circles and she decided there was nothing to do about that right now. So, she went back to the room, dressed quickly and grabbed her backpack.

She walked quickly down the sidewalk toward Lee Hall where her class had already started, and with each step her head pounded in unison with the pounding of the pavement. She reached to open the door to the building when she heard a voice behind her calling out her name. She turned quickly and immediately wished she had just kept going. Too late. There was Chris, jogging to catch up with her.

"Hey," he began, slightly out of breath.

"Hi," she replied. She looked down at her shoes, unable to look him in the eye.

"Listen, I know it's awkward between us. I know things are different now. Maybe they can't ever go back to the way things were, but I at least want to know we are okay." He sounded so sincere, Kelly couldn't help but look up.

"Well, I guess we are. I don't know if I am, but I think we are. Does that make sense?"

"Yeah. It makes sense. I really struggled at first, Kelly. But I have found some hope. I'd like to tell you about it."

"Well, maybe we can get together sometime. Not now. I'm not ready yet. But sometime," she replied as she reached once again to open the door.

"I understand," he replied. "Just let me know when you're ready," he said with a kind smile.

Kelly returned the smile, though hers was one mixed with great sadness. "Thanks, Chris. We'll talk soon." And with those parting words, she entered the building and walked quickly to her class.

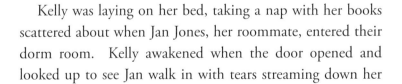

Kelly was laying on her bed, taking a nap with her books scattered about when Jan Jones, her roommate, entered their dorm room. Kelly awakened when the door opened and looked up to see Jan walk in with tears streaming down her cheeks.

Kelly sat up quickly and moved the books over so Jan could sit down. "What's wrong?" she asked with concern.

"Kelly, there is something I need to tell you," she began.

There was something about the tone of her voice which made Kelly's heart begin to pound, and a sense of impending doom came quickly upon her. "What? What happened?" she asked urgently.

"There was an accident, Kelly. It was a car wreck on Highway 82. It's Chris. He didn't make it," she said as she reached out to hug Kelly.

Kelly sat frozen on her bed, unable to feel the comfort Jan offered. "What? That can't be. I just saw him. We were going to talk." Her voice trailed off, and she felt trapped in a world of disbelief. And then the tears began. She and Jan sobbed together for a moment before Kelly got up, slipped on her shoes, and ran out the door. She didn't have a plan of where to go, she just had to run. She had to outrun the pain. In all her years of struggle, she still had not learned that you can't outrun pain.

CHAPTER

16

Kelly slipped in the church and slid into the first available seat—an aisle seat two rows from the back. She almost didn't come. She was torn between remembering Chris as the friend who always had her back and remembering him as the accomplice who led her to the worst decision of her life—the one she could never take back, never get over. She wanted to be there to honor him and their friendship, but that meant she had to face the onslaught of memories which threatened to drown her like the waves of a hurricane. In the end, the years of friendship outweighed the moments of mistakes and she rode alone to his hometown for the funeral. She looked in the seats closer to the front and recognized rows and rows of Mississippi State students, all of whom looked shell-shocked. She saw his roommate roughly wipe his eyes as well as the two freshman girls who were with Chris at The Grill the day she found out she was pregnant. A strange feeling of resentment passed over her when she saw the girls. *What are they doing here?* She thought angrily. *They hardly knew him at all. And they are crying as if they have a place here, as if they had history with him.* Her heart pounded in anger. *They didn't have* history with him. *But I did,* she thought as the anger turned to sadness. *I had history with him that no one else will ever know. And with his death, I have lost the only person who might have understood—who could have at least imagined what torment I feel. Because I know he felt it too—at least at first.*

The music from the organ began and sweet chord of comfort prompted friends and family to sing with conviction and hope.

Amazing Grace, how sweet the sound
That saved a wretch like me.
I once was lost but now I'm found.
Was blind but now I see.

A middle age man then rose from the front pew and walked to the pulpit. He cleared his throat, obviously struggling with emotion.

"I am David Willis, area director for Campus Crusade. I am a relatively new friend of Chris's, but I have a perspective on his life that his family wanted me to share with you. You see Chris was always a good guy. He was kind and patient. He respected authority and showed honor to his parents. He was a model son and friend. But I also know that standing before the throne of the King of kings as a 'good guy' won't get you very far. Chris was more than a good guy. He was a redeemed son of the Living God. A couple of months ago, Chris sought me out with questions to which he wanted answers. And praise God; I had the answers for him because I had searched for them myself many years ago. Deep down, Chris knew he needed a Savior. Deep down, he knew his 'good deeds' were like filthy rags before a holy and perfect God. And so we talked and we prayed and Chris found the answers he sought. He told me the past few months were some of the hardest he had ever experienced, but he was glad for those times because they brought him to relationship with the One who really mattered, Jesus Christ. Let me tell you what Chris is experiencing right now. I'm reading from Revelation 21:3-5. *And I heard a loud voice from the throne saying, 'Look! God's dwelling place is now among the people, and he will dwell with them. They will be his people, and God himself will be with them and be their God. 'He will wipe every tear from their eyes. There will be no more death' or mourning or crying or pain, for the old order of things has passed away.' He who was seated on the throne said, 'I am making everything new!' Then he said, 'Write this down, for these words are trustworthy and true.'"*

As David read the words of comfort about heaven, Kelly felt longing rising up in her soul. Though she had heard these words before, they never applied to her in the way they did at that moment.

"Our God gives us many promises in His Word, my friends. And every one is trustworthy and true. Chris is experiencing that truth right now. And for this we can rejoice, even through our tears. For we know that one day, God will also wipe away the tears from our eyes, just as Chris has experienced. And though our hearts are heavy with grief, we do not grieve without hope. This is what Chris would want you all to know. There is hope. And he found it."

With those final words, David returned to his seat and all were invited to rise and sing another hymn full of words of eternal hope.

Throughout David's speech, Kelly listened intently. She wanted to latch on to those words and never let go. She knew the words indeed were trustworthy and true, and she had no doubt that Chris was experiencing heavenly freedom from all which still chained her heart. She wanted this truth for her own life. For the first time since she was a young girl, she thought maybe this truth could change and heal her, just as it had done for Chris. She felt hope rise in her heart and though sorrowful tears streamed down her cheeks, she felt just a glimmer of joy. *Such a strange thing to feel at this moment*, she thought.

Just as she was about to give herself over to the release of this truth, she heard a tiny cry from the front right section reserved for the family. And there on the end of the row sat a cousin of Chris's, one whom Kelly had met before. And this cousin held her brand new baby and comforted the child, as the high-pitched cries grew louder, blending a strange melody with the sound of the congregation's song. And as the infant's cries grew louder, so did the words of accusation in Kelly's heart and head—words similar to what she heard outside the clinic that fateful day, words which stripped her of the tiny bit of hope and joy trying to take root in her heart. And she did what came naturally to her. She ran. She ran out of the church, vowing to never return. She could not be helped. She could not be healed. And she would never again be fooled into thinking she could.

CHAPTER

17

Time heals all wounds, or so they say. Maybe "heals" is not the right word. Maybe "dulls" or "hides" or "squashes" are words more accurately placed in the old adage. At least that is what Kelly experienced.

Through the next years, Kelly settled into a new identity. She was the party girl. Her coping habits turned into simply habits, or so she thought. She didn't know she was still running from pain, she just thought it was who she now was. The party girl. She was the fun one, the wild one, the unpredictable one. She didn't intend on becoming the party girl. It just was what it was. And she accepted this new identity with gusto and exuberance and rarely did she even feel guilty about it. Rarely did she dream of babies or loud machines or evil men who hurt little girls. Rarely did she think of her old friend, Chris. It all seemed like another life ago—as if it had all happened in the life of another girl, one who cared, maybe one she met in a dream long ago. This new girl didn't care, at least wouldn't let herself care. And so, she managed to laugh her way through college and land a job in Jackson, Mississippi.

Ironically, the girl who didn't care, chose a very caring

occupation. She got a degree in social work and her first job was counseling troubled kids in the public school system. She loved her job and she loved the children she counseled. She could allow herself to cry for them, for their pain. She just couldn't allow herself to cry for her own.

One day after arriving home from work, the phone in her apartment rang. She was tired and was tempted to let the answering machine get it, but on the last ring she ran and picked it up to answer. Her dad was on the other line and the sound of his voice brought tenderness to her icy heart.

"Hey, Honey. How's the job going?" he asked with sincerity.

The years of communicating with Sadie had taught Will the value of patience. He patiently waited to hear as many details as Kelly was willing to share. And she did share details. Even after all the years away, she knew the importance of sharing details. Her mother would be anxious to hear every last one, as if they were a lifeline between the two of them—between the life Sadie lived confined to her bed and the life Kelly lived, young and free to go and do and be. Of course, there were so many details Kelly could not—would not—share. But she could share about her job and the students, and so she did.

After Kelly had exhausted every tidbit she could think to share, her father spoke again. "Kel, I will be coming to Jackson next weekend for a college class reunion. After the big event in the Bowl and the football game following, our old group of friends will gather with our families at the Reservoir for a few hours. We are meeting at Goshen Springs campground at three in the afternoon. I was wondering if you would go with me?"

Kelly could hear the veiled pleading in his voice. She

knew he hated to go to these events without Sadie, and yet he always agreed to go so he could bring back news of their friends, which Sadie longed to hear. Normally, the thought of going to a gathering of her parents' college friends brought unbearable anxiety for Kelly. Aunt Rose and Uncle Al were sure to attend these events and seeing those two triggered the nightmares she had worked her whole life to overcome.

Though Kelly had never shared her nightmare with either of her parents, her father mentioned a couple of years back that Uncle Al had been diagnosed with Parkinson's disease. Kelly never asked for an update, but her father had recently mentioned that Al had greatly deteriorated in the past few months. Kelly tried hard not to be glad of that news, but she was. She wanted him to suffer at least as much as she had suffered due to his wicked, inexcusable schemes.

Feeling confident she would not have to see Rose or Al, Kelly agreed to go.

"Sure, Dad. I'll go with you," she replied, though her heart beat wildly in her chest.

"Oh, Honey, that's great! I can't wait to see you. Do you want to just meet me there?" he asked with genuine excitement.

"Sounds great. Tell Mom hi for me. I love you, Dad," she replied. She hung up the phone, staring into space for just a moment. She felt sure she would soon see Uncle Al in her nightmares.

The day of the college reunion arrived. Kelly drove with both hands on the steering wheel, knuckles white, teeth clenched. She was excited to see her dad, but anxious that the onslaught of memories may overtake her. She had attended many other such reunions over the years, and had spent each one hiding from Uncle Al. Though she was sure he would not attend due to his health limitations, the memories alone made her want to turn the car around and flee to the safety of her apartment or the local bar. But she pressed onward driving down Highway 55 until she came to the Natchez Trace exit. She drove fifteen minutes down the Trace, enough time to let the tension ease out of her body and enjoy the beauty of the drive.

The Natchez Trace Parkway begins in Nashville, Tennessee, and ends in Natchez, Mississippi. It is beautiful with its array of pine, poplar, and oak trees framing the narrow drive. The beauty of the Trace is to be savored, thus a special team of highway patrolmen strictly protect the speed limit. Kelly spotted a patrolman and instinctively slammed on her brakes. She lowered her speed, avoided a ticket, and soon saw the flickering specks of sunlight reflecting off the massive body of water which formed the Reservoir. The western shore of the Reservoir is bounded by the Trace, and Kelly drove several miles enjoying the scene to her right before she found the turn to the campground chosen for the reunion.

The Ross Barnett Reservoir—also known as "The Rez"—is a containment of the Pearl River, which forms the 33,000-acre lake. Kelly's destination was the pavilion at Goshen Springs Campground. They would grill hamburgers and hotdogs, fish from the dock, and swim in the pool. Kelly intentionally brought neither swim suit nor fishing gear so she could keep her stay brief and make an easy get away if her anxiety levels grew unbearable.

She easily found the campground and pulled into a parking spot under the shade of a huge oak tree. The afternoon September sun was still hot in this central part of Mississippi, and though school was in full swing, it still felt like summertime. Kelly parked and opened the door to experience a gush of hot humid air. By the time she had walked the short distance to the pavilion, she was glistening with perspiration and had already swatted at mosquitoes threatening to feast on her long, tan legs. *I should have at least brought bug spray*, she thought.

She quickly spotted her dad talking to an old friend who had settled on the Coast—the opposite direction of Tupelo. She walked up and hugged her dad and was quickly re-introduced.

"Kelly, you remember Sam, don't you?" her dad asked pleasantly.

"Yes, sir. Mr. Sam, it is good to see you again!" Kelly replied with the exuberance of a typical southern young lady.

"Kelly, you are looking well! My daughter, Megan, is here. I know you two have hit it off at past gatherings. The last time I saw her she was headed to the pier."

"Oh, great! I didn't know she would be here. We have kept up over the years. I will go down there and try to find her," she replied. She turned and kissed her dad on the cheek and then headed toward the water.

Kelly quickly caught up with Megan and they stopped at the nearest picnic table to talk. Megan was a petite, fair strawberry blond, which contrasted drastically to Kelly's tall and tan features. But their personalities were similar even if their physical features were vastly different. Though they had only seen each other face to face a handful of times, they both seemed drawn together in friendship, as if they had known each other day in and day out for their entire lives. Conversation came easily and the usual pretense of a casual friend was never a barrier between them.

After an hour of non-stop talking, they agreed to continue down to the water. They walked further through the wooded area and broke through to the open, grassy hill. The late afternoon sun reflected on the water and burst around the few clouds in wonderful brilliance. The temperature seemed cooler and pleasant voices from the water's edge wafted up the hill. Suddenly, Megan stopped walking and stood very still. Her eyes were glued to the pier and the group of people gathered there. Kelly silently followed the path of Megan's gaze and the sight made her heart beat faster. An old man in a wheelchair had made his way to the edge of the pier, obviously helped there by one of the men standing near by. It was Uncle Al. Kelly noticed his slumped position in the wheelchair, and as she watched she saw him try to control the shaking movements long enough to scratch his head. After several tries of misplaced landings, his hand shakily scratched the spot. The small gesture seemed to exhaust him and he slumped even further in his wheelchair. Kelly felt frozen to the particular spot of grass where they had stopped and was so caught up in her focus of the scene before her, she almost forgot Megan was by her side. That is, until Megan spoke.

Her normal bubbly voice was low and chillingly quiet as she said, "I'd like to roll him right into the water."

Kelly spun her head quickly toward Megan, though Megan never let her eyes move from the man in the wheelchair.

"You, too?" Kelly asked timidly, her voice slightly trembling.

Megan turned toward Kelly with tears welling up in her eyes. She nodded, but still didn't speak. Neither said a word as they sat on the grass. Misery and comfort wrapped up together, and for the first time in forever, Kelly did not feel alone in her pain.

CHAPTER

18

Five-year-old Tessa pulled a chair flush to the kitchen counter. She grabbed the arm of the chair and pulled her little body up to the seat. She stood on the chair dressed in a tiny T-shirt and undies decorated with the characters from Rug Rats, the children's program which she watched daily. The metal "rabbit ears" on top of the bulky television set did not always pick up the best picture, but Tessa had learned that Rug Rats came on in the morning when she woke up and in the afternoon when her mom slept. She had learned to adjust the "rabbit ears" by pulling them wider or by squeezing the aluminum foil balls on the ends of each metal rod.

Tessa continued in her mission as she placed a skinny leg on the counter and pulled herself up by holding onto the edge of the sink. Once securely on top of the counter, she was free to walk its length opening all the cabinets, searching for a can of Popeye canned spinach. Finding what she was looking for, she climbed back down with the can tucked under her chin.

When she reached the floor, she walked over to the utensil

drawer and pulled it open. She was slightly taller than the drawer, though she couldn't see inside, so she felt around until she found the can opener. She placed the can on the floor and then placed the can opener wide on the can. With as much weight as she could muster, she pushed the handles shut until she heard the faint wisp of air, which indicated the can opener was lodged in place. Now came the hard part. She grasped the knob and twisted bit by bit until she had made enough of an opening to pull the contents out with the fork she had also retrieved from the utensil drawer. She sat on the floor and pulled the wet strands of cold spinach from the small opening in the can.

Most children her age would have refused spinach as the main (and only) course for dinner. Tessa, however, had grown to love it. She felt proud of herself for figuring out how to feed herself. Now that she was a "big girl" she didn't have to bother her mom to help her. This accomplishment brought relief from the irritable rants from her mother and the tears of the child. Tessa loved when her mom patted her head with a limp hand and groggily whispered, "That's my big girl" before she closed her eyes in sleep again.

Tessa had figured out that when the bottle on the bed was empty, there was no use trying to get her mother's attention. She would not wake up, no matter how loud she cried. And in the resilient manner of children, Tessa had found a way to take care of herself and achieve the occasional word of affirmation from her mother. She happily ate her spinach and thought of the time her mother told her about Popeye. Her mom was very alert that day and seemed eager to sit with Tessa on the couch and tell her stories of her own childhood.

"When I was little, my favorite show was Popeye the Sailor Man," her mom reminisced.

"Why didn't you watch Rug Rats," Tessa asked.

"Well, that was before Rug Rats was created," her mom replied as she hugged her close. "Actually, Popeye was an old show when I was little. But you could still watch it as re-runs. I think I liked it because my mom said it was her favorite," she said dreamily. She looked straight ahead as she spoke this last statement, as if she was trying to recount the details of a dream she once had.

"I want to watch Popeye the Sailor Man. It will be my favorite, too!" Tessa replied eagerly.

"You can't watch it now, Tessa. It doesn't come on anymore. Maybe we can find a VHS tape one day. Roy and Silvia have a video player. Maybe they would let us borrow it, if we find the tape," Tammy replied.

At the sound of Roy's name, Tessa scooted closer to Tammy. Roy scared her, and he seemed to enjoy it. She had told her mother she was scared of him, but her mother told her there was no need to be afraid. "Roy and Silvia take care of us. They let us live here for free. You be nice to them, Tessa. I don't want you to mess things up," her mother had replied. And so, Tessa tried to be nice, but she stayed as far away from Roy as she could.

Tammy never bought a Popeye video, but she did start buying Popeye canned spinach. It had been Tessa's favorite ever since.

Two years later, Tessa got off the school bus at the top

of the hill. She waved to the bus driver, Ms. Walker, and skipped down the road to the driveway. The roar of the bus grew fainter and fainter as she neared the property where she lived. She walked carefully down the steep gravel drive until she reached the rickety steps of the trailer. As she reached the landing, she noticed a rip in the screen door. "No wonder the mosquitos have been biting me," she thought.

As she reached for the door handle, she stopped cold, as the deep sound of a man's voice wafted through the screen. It was Roy. She lowered her hand and quietly laid her Hello Kitty backpack on the landing. She tip-toed down the three steps and slipped under the porch. She decided to sit quietly under the steps until he left. She could still hear the two voices—wait, maybe it was three. *Yes, that's Silvia*, Tessa thought. She relaxed a bit at the sound of Silvia's voice. Roy was not so scary when Silvia was around.

"That Tessa is a pretty one," Roy said with an eerie chuckle. A shiver went down Tessa's spine. She strained to hear her mother's response, but the weaker voice was faint and muffled.

"We could put Tessa to work. She's old enough now. She could deliver things for us. It could take place at the park. Would look like a normal kid playing," he said. Tessa heard more muffled words from her mom, but the harsh response from Roy indicated he was not happy with her comments.

"This is my trailer and my property. And it is my supply that keeps you happy. Remember that," he said angrily as he opened the screen and slammed it behind him.

He stomped down the wooden steps, never noticing Tessa underneath. Soon after, softer footsteps came down the stairs, and Tessa watched Silvia walk quickly down the road trying to catch up with Roy. When Tessa could no longer see the two through the slats of the steps, she rose from her hiding spot and made her way inside the trailer. Her mother was already in bed, with the door closed. Tessa pushed a chair to the counter, climbed up, and retrieved another can of Popeye spinach.

CHAPTER

19

Tammy tossed and turned in the bed. The sheets grew tangled, and the thin mattress pad lost its grip on the rounded corners of the mattress. The empty glass bottle crashed to the floor, the sound of which awakened Tammy from her terrifying dreams.

Tammy sat up quickly in bed. Her head pounded and sweat dripped down the sides of her temples. Her heart raced and she thought she might be sick. She lay back down hoping to calm the rapid beating of her heart.

Just breathe, she told herself. *It was only a dream.* Scenes flitted through her mind as she remembered and re-lived her nightmare. The darkness of the room was nothing compared to the darkness of her dream. Dark and terrifying. And Roy was the main character.

Shaking, she turned on her side, as tears fell from her eyes mixing with the moisture of the perspiration on the pillow. *I've got to get Tessa out of here,* she thought in desperation.

It was Friday afternoon. The November sky was overcast but the grey backdrop only highlighted the yellow, red, and brown leaves still hanging on the trees. A cool breeze blew Tessa's brown, straight hair across her eyes. She reached up to brush it back as she made her way quickly to the trailer. She couldn't wait to get home and tell her mom about her day. *If she is awake, that is.*

She opened the door to the trailer and saw that though her mom was in her bed, the door to the bedroom was open, which Tessa interpreted as an invitation in.

Tammy seemed more alert than usual, so Tessa hopped up on the bed and sat closely next to her mother, who extended her arm for a hug.

"How was your day?" Tammy asked with sincerity.

"It was great! I couldn't wait to tell you! Mary asked me to spend the night tonight. Can I, please?" she begged.

"Who's Mary," Tammy asked.

"Mary. My best friend. Remember? I sit by her in class," Tessa replied impatiently.

"Well, I guess it's okay. When am I supposed to take you? You know, I will have to clear it with Roy to borrow the car."

"She said to call her if I can come. I wrote down her phone number. It's in my backpack," Tessa replied excitedly. "So, I can go?" she squealed.

"Yes, you can go. As long as it's okay with Roy. We can walk down now and ask him, then call from there. If he says it's okay, we will leave right away, so go grab your stuff," Tammy replied. She smiled as Tessa skipped to the back of the trailer. For just a moment, Tammy felt like a normal mom.

The Saturday sunset was beautiful as the two girls swung on the play set in Mary's backyard. "Girls, come in for supper," Mary's mom yelled from the back door. They entered the house and at Mary's instruction, ran to the kitchen to wash their hands. The smell of spaghetti and French bread made Tessa's tummy growl. She spotted the chocolate chip cookies on the counter and smiled. *Yum*, she thought in anticipation.

After saying the blessing over the food, the family dug in to the delicious meal. Mary's mom cast a glance toward her husband before she spoke. "Tessa, did your mom say anything to you about her plans for the weekend? I haven't been able to get in touch with her."

"No, ma'am," she answered sweetly, with her mouth full of noodles.

"Do you know if she had our phone number?"

"Yes, ma'am. I left it on the counter in the kitchen. It had Mary's name on it with your number," Tessa replied. She had been having so much fun, she had not even thought about her mother. However, the looks exchanged between Mary's parents made her nervous. Suddenly, the spaghetti didn't taste so good.

Mary's mother noticed the worried look on Tessa's face, and quickly reassured her. "Don't worry, Honey. I will try again after dinner. If we can't get in touch with her, you can just spend another night. Wouldn't that be fun?"

Thinking it would indeed be fun, Tessa took another big bite of spaghetti, not bothering to wipe the sauce from her chin.

On Sunday morning, Tessa borrowed a dress from Mary and went to church for the first time ever. She loved Sunday school with all the songs, games, and crafts. The church service, however, was long and boring and Tessa was glad when it was over. As they drove home from church, Mary's mother cast another glance at her husband and began asking questions once again.

"Tessa, do you have any other family in town?"

"Yes, ma'am. My grandmother lives here. We don't see her very often, though," Tessa replied honestly.

"Do you know her phone number?" Mary's mother asked.

"No ma'am," Tessa replied.

"Do you know her name?"

"Oh, yes, ma'am. Her name is Ruth. Ruth Thomas," Tessa obliged. She was happy to have an answer for Mary's mom.

It was another beautiful afternoon, and Mary and Tessa spent most of it playing outside. They rode bikes around the cul-de-sac, played on the play set, and drew pictures on the sidewalk with chalk. They were playing in the front yard, as the sun once again began its descent behind the trees, when a white car pulled into the driveway. Tessa looked up and saw her grandmother get out of the car.

"Tessa, go get your stuff," she said flatly. "And hurry up!" she commanded.

Tessa didn't go to the trailer that night, or the next one either. In fact, Tessa rarely went back to the trailer after that weekend.

CHAPTER

20

Kelly rolled over in bed and each movement brought searing pain to her head. She felt a wave of nausea sweep over her and she lifted her head slightly to find the location of the trash can, just in case she needed it—which was likely. Scenes rolled through her head like clips from movie previews, and she wasn't sure which scenes were true memories. Dancing and drinking in excess were the general themes of each scene.

After a few minutes of being utterly still, she mustered the courage to roll over on her side in order to see the alarm clock on the table beside her bed. 7:15 am. *There is no way I can make it to work today. I'll have to call in sick—again.* She felt like a failure. She knew the children were counting on her, but she had failed them once again.

She picked up the phone by her bed and dialed the number to the school office. She didn't have to pretend to sound sick, she really was. But the raw truth was the "sickness" could have been avoided if only she had a little discretion and self-control.

"Hello, Northside Elementary. How may I help you?"

"Hello, Mrs. Boone, this is Kelly Humphrey." Momentary

silence. When Mrs. Boone spoke again, her normally cheerful voice was greatly altered.

"Yes, Kelly?" she asked coldly.

Kelly cringed but continued on with the purpose of her call. "Um. Well, I'm really sick this morning. I won't be able to come in for work today," she replied weakly.

Another momentary silence. "Well, I will tell Mr. Jenkins," she said. After a brief pause, she spoke again. Though her words were those of reprimand, they were also a bit softer. "Kelly, this may be none of my business. But I really like you and would hate for you to lose your job. This has got to stop. Mr. Jenkins is running low on patience. You cannot keep calling in sick. You may not feel well, but sometimes you must press on. Go to a doctor—or a counselor—and get help. Otherwise, you will lose your job."

"Yes, ma'am," Kelly replied meekly. Both hung up without saying goodbye. *Well, they are on to me*, Kelly thought. She wanted to be casual about it, laugh it away, and act like she didn't care. But she did care. Tears streamed down her cheeks, first like a gentle rain, then like a fierce storm. The black clouds in her soul had been rumbling and rolling for so long, they were bound to break open at some point. And this was it. She sobbed until the emotion mixed with her hangover caused her to race to the bathroom. After she lost the remaining contents of her supper, she hung over the sink trying to wash away the nausea and the shame. When she looked in the mirror, she didn't recognize the face before her. Anger rose up forcefully and she felt pure hatred for the reflection she saw. In an act of rage, she picked up her boot, discarded in a heap the night before and sent it sailing heel first into the hated image of the mirror. The mirror cracked down the middle causing ugly,

A Broken Mirror

broken lines in her reflection. She stood and stared at the broken mirror, rage quickly replaced by deep despair.

Afterwards, she lay back down on the bed and let the flow of tears loose once again. Loud cries came from the deep places she had carefully controlled, and briefly she wondered if her apartment neighbors could hear her. After several moments of uncontrollable sobbing, Kelly began to pray aloud. She raised her arms toward the sky, reaching up in desperation.

"God, if You are there, I need help. I know I don't have any right to come to You. I have rejected you for so long. But I do believe in You, God. And if you will help me, I will be so grateful. I don't know where to turn. I don't know how to get out of this mess. I don't know how to pull myself together. Please help me. I'm sorry, God. So sorry. If You are there, please send me one friend. One Christian friend, God."

Kelly rolled over and continued to cry until her pillow was wet with moisture of desperation and her body and mind found the temporary relief of troubled sleep.

Two weeks later, Kelly stepped onto the only available treadmill and began to warm up with fast-paced steps before she began her two-mile trek. Going to the gym near her apartment was part of Kelly's new resolve to pull herself together. She had also not had a single drink since the day of her "breaking" as she liked to think of it. Yes, she had broken, but she pressed forward hoping she was on the road to recovery. She glanced to the right at the girl jogging next to her. Both smiled and then continued looking straight ahead out the window as they ran in place. Later, Kelly saw the girl again in the women's locker room. Both smiled once again, and the girl introduced herself as Hope.

"Have you just started coming here, Kelly?" Hope asked as she gathered her things and placed them back in her gym bag.

"Yes. I'm trying to get back in shape," Kelly replied pleasantly.

"Well, you look like you are already in shape," Hope observed. "I come here just about everyday. It was nice to meet you. I hope to see you soon," she said as she grabbed her gym bag and headed out the door.

Oddly, the words of her prayer came to mind as she watched Hope leave the locker room. "If You are there, please send me one friend. One Christian friend, God." And Kelly prayed that prayer once again.

Two months later, Kelly and Hope finished two miles on the treadmill in sync. "Let's try the elliptical," Kelly said.

"I would love to, but I have Bible Study. But why don't you come with me?" Hope replied.

"Oh, I don't know," Kelly stalled.

"Come on. It's fun, I promise. It's a small group of really nice people. I think you would enjoy it. I promise they won't ask you to pray out loud," she said with a smile.

Kelly thought for just a moment before replying. God had answered her prayers by sending Hope just when she needed a good friend. *I guess the least I could do is give it a try*, she thought. "That would be great. I'd like to go," she said to Hope with a peaceful resolve she had not felt in many years. And thus began a season of healing, and ever so slowly, Kelly began to trust once again—both God and man.

CHAPTER

21

Kelly opened the passenger car door, suddenly wishing she had brought her own car. She wanted the safety of a "getaway car" if she didn't feel comfortable at the Bible Study. Hope seemed to sense her nervousness, and stuck close by her side as they walked up the stairs of the church. As they opened the heavy door, the silence and smell of the place brought back a flood of memories, most of which seemed like the flowing shadows of a happy dream. She had spent many hours in a church much like the one she now entered. She could even vaguely recall the times she was at the church with her mother—whole and healthy at that time.

Hope whispered to her as they walked down the corridor. There was really no need to whisper, but the environment seemed to evoke a reverent hush.

"I grew up in this church," Hope said quietly. "I accepted Christ when I was nine years old. Right there in that Sunday School room," she said as she pointed to a brightly colored door with a window in the middle. They paused just a moment to look inside. Colorful posters hung on the wall depicting various scenes from the Old and New Testaments. Kelly's gaze fell on the poster of Noah.

As they silently continued down the hallway, Kelly's thoughts continued to review the story of Noah. *Wickedness. Wrath. Flood. Death. Why do they teach this to kids? Why are all the animals cute, and why is Noah always depicted as happy?* She thought randomly.

Her musings were suddenly interrupted as they arrived at their destination. Hope confidently opened the door as Kelly nervously wiped her sweaty hands on her jeans. Inside, a dozen or so young adults mingled around a table laden with Cokes, chips, and dip. Kelly smiled as Hope took her to each cluster of people and introduced her as her "dear friend". This title caused Kelly to relax a bit, and she felt thankful once again that God had answered her prayer through Hope.

The leader called the group to sit closely together on the mismatched couches, which formed a circle on the far side of the spacious room. Hope volunteered to open the group in prayer, and Kelly was amazed with the easy way she spoke— as if she were speaking to a friend, not the Creator of the Universe.

The minister, a middle-aged man named Richard, told the group to open their Bibles to the book of Genesis. Kelly suddenly felt embarrassed. *Why didn't I think to bring a Bible to Bible Study?* she thought. *Not that I have one at my apartment.* Her embarrassment quickly dissipated when Hope scooted closer to her and shared her open Bible. Kelly smiled just a bit as the irony of the day's topic was revealed.

"Okay, guys. Today, I want to take you back to your Sunday School days," Richard began. "Our topic is Noah. We all know the story of Noah and the great flood. After many years of seeing the wickedness of the earth, God had finally had enough. It was time for a great cleansing. Cleansing away the evil was the only way to save the earth. Noah was the only righteous man left, and it was said of him that he 'walked with God.' What a beautiful picture of a faithful follower—simply walking with God."

At that moment, Kelly thought of her dad. She thought of how his faith had remained solid during all the years of hardship. She thought of how he lovingly and faithfully took care of Sadie, and suddenly she realized he had never complained. *I have never heard him complain, not once,* she thought as tears welled up in her eyes. She lowered her eyes so no one would notice and pretended as if she were looking at the words in the Bible.

"Noah and his family were the sole survivors of the great flood and the recipients of the covenant promise God made to never again destroy the earth by flood. The sign of this covenant, or never-ending promise, is the rainbow. This is usually where the Sunday School version stops. But let's dig a little deeper. Noah had three sons, Ham, Shem, and Japheth. In Genesis 9, we see a brief but important story concerning Noah and these three sons. Stan, would you mind reading that passage aloud? Genesis 9:18-23."

A brief silence followed as Stan Williams found the passage in his well-worn open Bible. Kelly glanced over and noticed for the first time this tall, handsome twenty-three year old young man. *Strong, silent type*, she thought. He had not said a word before this moment and had sat in a chair in the corner, behind the couches. Though she had not met him yet, he exuded depth and strength and confidence which were wrapped up neatly in the covering of humility, like a precious gift wrapped in beautiful paper—the type that is almost too nice to open. And though Kelly definitely liked what she saw, words of accusation quickly assaulted her. *A guy like that would never want a girl like me.* And once again she looked down at the open Bible, her face pink with shame.

Stan's voice was much like his countenance—strong, clear, and easy to understand. He read the following passage without a single stumble over the words or the names, and Kelly felt sure he had read many such passages aloud.

"*The sons of Noah who came out of the ark were Shem, Ham and Japheth. (Ham was the father of Canaan.) These were the three sons of Noah, and from them came the people who were scattered over the earth.*

Noah, a man of the soil, proceeded to plant a vineyard. When he drank some of its wine, he became drunk and lay uncovered inside his tent. Ham, the father of Canaan, saw his father's nakedness and told his two brothers outside. But Shem and Japheth took a garment and laid it across their shoulders; then they walked in backward and covered their father's nakedness. Their faces were turned the other way so that they would not see their father's nakedness."

"Thanks, Stan," Richard said, then added with a twinkle in his eye, "Don't worry, guys, this is not a message about the evils of alcohol." Everyone laughed at this and Kelly was secretly thankful she would not have to endure that topic of discussion.

Richard continued, "It is unclear here whether Noah purposely became intoxicated; however, he was very drunk and in this state lay unconscious and naked inside his tent. Ham, the youngest, was the first to discover Noah in this awkward position. When Ham saw his father, he did not cover his shame, but instead broadcast it to the others. Shem and Japheth, on the other hand, took a garment and laid it across their shoulders and walked in backwards. Not only did they refuse to broadcast their father's sin and shame, but they also had compassion and covered it.

There are important lessons for us in this brief account. First of all, how do we respond to the sin and shame of those around us? Do we look on the shame and sin of others and broadcast it to the world through gossip and judgment? Or do we handle the mistakes of others with privacy and covering? I am not talking about keeping secrets. Secrets can be dangerous things."

Kelly immediately thought of all the times she had wanted to tell the dark secrets buried in her heart and memory, and briefly thought, *Maybe it would help to lay it all out—every bit of it.* And instinctively she once again lowered her head in shame.

"And I am not talking about ignoring sin or having a 'free to be you and me' attitude concerning sin," Richard continued. "We are called to speak truth, but Ephesians 4:15 says to speak truth in love. Let's look at what else God's Word has to say. Holly, Beth, and Heath will you guys read the passages I gave you earlier?" One by one they each read one of the following passages of scripture.

"Hatred stirs up dissension, but love covers over all wrongs. Proverbs 10:12."

"He who covers over an offense promotes love, but whoever repeats the matter separates close friends. Proverbs 17:9."

"Above all, love each other deeply, because love covers over a multitude of sins. 1 Peter 4:8."

Richard continued, "We also find in Matthew 18:15 an outline for a Biblical approach to confronting others in their mistakes and in misunderstandings, and it doesn't involve an announcement to everyone we meet, even in the form of a 'prayer request.' That approach is called gossip, and it too is a sin. We all, including me, need to evaluate our first response to the sin and shame of others: Do we go to the phone or do we go to the Throne?" Quiet laughter reverberated around the room.

Maybe I could tell Richard, maybe I could trust him with my dark secrets. Maybe he wouldn't judge. Maybe he would help me, Kelly thought.

Kelly turned her attention back to Richard as he said, "The second lesson we can learn from this account concerns the action of honoring others. Honoring our father and mother, even when we are grown, is vital—so vital that it is included in the Ten Commandments and is the only commandment with a promise attached to it. 'Honor your father and your mother, as the LORD your God has commanded you, so that you may live long and that it may go well with you in the land the LORD your God is giving you.' Deuteronomy 5:16. In Genesis 5:1, Moses summoned all of Israel for these commandments. We tend to use this one to teach children to obey, but we must not forget that honoring our parents is a lifelong commandment."

A movie reel of mistakes flitted through Kelly's mind in no particular order, and for the first time in a very long time, she felt regret that she had not honored her parents. *They have always loved me and welcomed me, no matter what*, she thought.

"Ham did not honor his father, and the results were painful consequences for generations after. When Noah awoke from his wine and found out what his youngest son had done to him, he said, 'Cursed be Canaan! The lowest of slaves will he be to his brothers.' He also said, 'Blessed be the LORD, the God of Shem! May Canaan be the slave of Shem. May God extend the territory of Japheth; may Japheth live in the tents of Shem, and may Canaan be his slave.' Genesis 9:24-27."

"You see," Richard continued, "Canaan was one of Ham's sons. So Noah was saying that not only will Ham be cursed, but all the generations to come will be too. Noah also said, 'Blessed be the LORD, the God of Shem!' The glory in Shem's blessing was aimed at God, not Shem, because his reaction to sin and shame came from his understanding and respect for God. God got the glory for his righteous action. Shem was blessed because he represented God well by honoring his father and by covering his shame. For reasons unclear, Shem was the one most regarded for this event, perhaps because it was his idea to cover his father and not look upon his shame. Perhaps Japheth, when faced with the opposite opinions and actions of his two brothers, chose to stand with the righteous one, the brother who exhibited integrity. He too was blessed for it. The blessing was as follows: May Canaan be the slave of Shem. May God extend the territory of Japheth; may Japheth live in the tents of Shem, and may Canaan be his slave."

At this point, Kelly was a little confused. *What does this have to do with anything?* she thought.

"Let's stop for just a moment and address the elephant in the room," Richard continued. "Many of you may be thinking, God honored a curse that a father placed on his own son? That doesn't sound loving or fair or kind or just, does it? I confess that I struggled with that thought, too. But as I thought and prayed it through, I came to the following conclusions.

First of all, we have to remember the culture of those days. Blessings and curses were a part of life. For reasons hard for us to understand now, the blessing (or curse) of the father was vital and powerful, both in the physical realm and in the spiritual realm.

Second, we again have to remember the culture of those days. Honoring parents was a big deal back then. What Ham did was a big deal, because he dishonored his father. It doesn't seem like a big deal to us, but in those times and in that culture, it was a major offense."

"Third," Richard continued, "we have to remember the culture of the heavenly realm, which involves holiness. God is altogether holy. This big sin of Ham was not only an offense to Noah; it was also an offense to God. God cannot look upon sin. Sin is the huge chasm that separates us from God. And guess what? That has not changed. God is the same yesterday, today, and forever. His holiness has not changed. He still cannot look upon sin."

I guess I'm cursed, too. No surprise there, Kelly thought dejectedly.

"The curse stood because the sin remained, and it remained for the generations which came through Ham—the Canaanites. Next week we will study about how Shem's descendant, Abram, was called to take back the promise land from the Canaanites, because of the blessings promised during this encounter. But what I want you to understand right now is very important."

Richard paused just a moment and looked around the room. His eyes were serious, but kind—as if he longed for them to understand the truth he spoke. "If God has not changed, what has changed?" he continued. "Why don't we have to live in fear of the curse of sin and death?"

The room was silent until Stan's strong voice simply said,

"Because of Jesus and His work on the cross."

Richard smiled and pointed to Stan. "That's it! The answer lies in two verses I want us to look at. Jeff and Hilary, read those verses I gave you." And each read the assigned scripture.

"If a man guilty of a capital offense is put to death and his body is hung on a tree, you must not leave his body on the tree overnight. Be sure to bury him that same day, because anyone who is hung on a tree is under God's curse. Deuteronomy 21:22-23," Jeff read.

"Christ redeemed us from the curse of the Law, having become a curse for us--for it is written, 'Cursed is everyone who hangs on a tree.' Galatians 3:13," Hilary followed.

Richard smiled and took a deep breath, as if he was relieved to get to the good news of a difficult passage. "Jesus hung on the tree to take the curse for us. The holiness of God demanded that the curse be fulfilled. It is only through Jesus that the curse of sin and death is taken away from us because He fulfilled the curse on our behalf. Praise Him for this great news!"

Just after the last amen of the closing prayer, Kelly leaned over and whispered to Hope, "Do you think we could stay for a few minutes after everyone leaves? I have something I want to talk to Richard about." Hope nodded and smiled, and deep down she knew God was answering her prayers for her dear friend, Kelly.

CHAPTER

22

Kelly smiled at Mrs. Boone as she signed out at the school office. Mrs. Boone smiled back sincerely and asked, "Any plans for the weekend, Kelly? The weather is supposed to be really nice, you know."

"Yes, ma'am. Some friends from my Bible Study have invited me to go skiing at the Rez. I haven't been skiing in ages. I hope I don't break something!" she replied with a laugh.

"That will be fun! I love going out on our boat at the Rez. But my skiing days are long gone," she replied. Both laughed together in the soft way of good friends. Mrs. Boone paused just a moment and then spoke again, this time more seriously. "Kelly, I've been wanting to tell you something for months now," she paused until Kelly looked at her with full attention.

"Yes, ma'am?" Kelly asked. Dread took hold, causing her to hold her breath. *What have I done now?* She thought as she racked her brain trying to anticipate Mrs. Boone's next words.

"I'm very proud of you," Mrs. Boone simply said looking intently in Kelly's eyes. They both smiled. Kelly had indeed made an about-face. Everything in her life had changed in the past months, and Kelly was both happy and relieved she was in this place at this time in her life. She tried hard not to look back, simply forward to all God had planned for her life.

"Thank you, Mrs. Boone," Kelly replied with sincerity. "I have a lot to be thankful for."

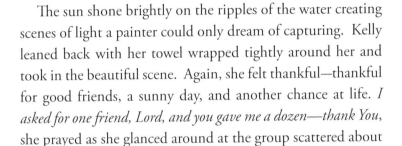

The sun shone brightly on the ripples of the water creating scenes of light a painter could only dream of capturing. Kelly leaned back with her towel wrapped tightly around her and took in the beautiful scene. Again, she felt thankful—thankful for good friends, a sunny day, and another chance at life. *I asked for one friend, Lord, and you gave me a dozen—thank You*, she prayed as she glanced around at the group scattered about the pontoon boat. They had spent all afternoon on this boat, as well as the ski boat loaned to them by a generous church member. She sat next to Hope who sat next to Beth, who sat next to Holly. Across from them were Stan and Heath. Kelly had grown to love and appreciate all of her new friends and found them to be fun and genuine and "normal". They also happened to love Jesus with their whole hearts.

She was most impressed with Stan. She watched him when he wasn't aware of her gaze, and she learned a lot about him through observation. She found him to be kind to everyone, strong physically and spiritually, and a quiet servant to all. The fact that he was very handsome, too, was like icing on the cake.

She noticed all the little things which made up who he was like the way he took the tomatoes off his burger, without complaining that the waiter had forgotten his request; and how he bent down low to talk to the children at church. She noticed that he was always the first to jump up when someone needed help—and he didn't wait to be asked, either. He noticed what people needed and silently did what he could to meet those needs. And though he was quiet, when he did speak his words were wise and beneficial to whoever listened. After today, she realized he could make her laugh in a way that is pure and free. He glanced her way and they shared a smile and a look that lasted a bit longer than that of friendship. Kelly was the first to look away, and she gazed once again at the water and the sun dipping lower and lower on the horizon. *I'd better be careful*, Kelly thought, *or I could fall for Stan just as quickly as the sun is falling from the sky. I can see he likes me, too—and he deserves much better than me.* And that last thought was the one grey cloud in an otherwise perfect day.

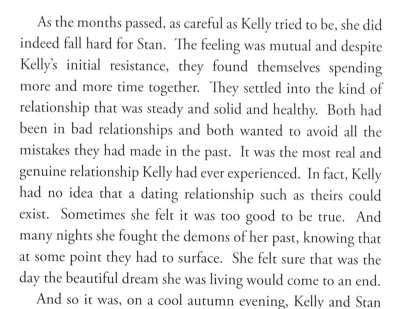

As the months passed, as careful as Kelly tried to be, she did indeed fall hard for Stan. The feeling was mutual and despite Kelly's initial resistance, they found themselves spending more and more time together. They settled into the kind of relationship that was steady and solid and healthy. Both had been in bad relationships and both wanted to avoid all the mistakes they had made in the past. It was the most real and genuine relationship Kelly had ever experienced. In fact, Kelly had no idea that a dating relationship such as theirs could exist. Sometimes she felt it was too good to be true. And many nights she fought the demons of her past, knowing that at some point they had to surface. She felt sure that was the day the beautiful dream she was living would come to an end.

And so it was, on a cool autumn evening, Kelly and Stan

sat comfortably on a park bench, sharing the minute details of their day. For a time, they sat in comfortable silence, enjoying the cool temperatures and gentle breeze which caused already loosened leaves of red and yellow and orange, to lose their grip and fall to the ground, forming puddles of color all over the park. Kelly turned and looked at Stan's profile and love welled up in her heart so fiercely, it brought tears to her eyes. *I have to tell him*, she thought suddenly. *He deserves to know.*

Just as she contemplated how she could possibly reveal her secrets to such a godly, perfect man, he turned and looked at her. He saw the tears forming puddles on her lower lids, sat up quickly, and turned to ask, "Kelly, what's wrong?" His concern was so genuine and his strong voice so gentle, the tears finally spilled over onto her face and fell softly down her cheeks. She didn't bother to wipe them away.

"Stan, I don't know what the future holds for us. And I'm not making assumptions about how you feel about me. But before we go much further in our relationship, there are some things you need to know. Things I need to tell you, that I wish more than anything I didn't have to share. But you deserve to know who I really am—past and present. And I am sad to say that the past me and the present me are two very different people." Kelly paused for a moment and squeezed her eyes shut causing more tears to flow down her face.

Stan took her hands into his and said, "Kelly, look at me." She looked up miserably and felt once again the overwhelming love for him, mixed with the knowledge she was about to lose that love. He pulled one hand away from hers and reached up to gently wipe away the steady flow of tears.

"I only want to know one thing about your past, Kelly," he said in a low and serious manner. *Here it comes*, she thought.

This is when he finds out who I really am. Lord, please let me just tell the truth. Keep my tongue from lies, Lord, she prayed silently.

"Has God forgiven you?" he asked. He looked intently at her face to gauge her response.

"Yes. I know He has," she replied with a confidence which was new to her but very much a part of who she now was.

"Then so do I," Stan replied, as he pulled her close and kissed the top of her head while her tears of relief formed wet rings on his shirt.

And that night was the night she knew. Incredulous as it seemed, God was blessing her—even her—with far more than she could have ever imagined.

CHAPTER

23

Sadie closed her eyes as the cassette tape cast the soothing sounds for her to savor. Each word meant so much to Sadie. She had always loved God, for as long as she could remember. Her father taught her early in life the joy of savoring hymns as an act of worship. She had not understood the significance of the lyrics of some of those songs until she was so desperate in her need of Him. She had not known until her diagnosis that deep despair could usher in deep dependence on the One who had saved her soul. And that deep dependence could usher in a peace and joy beyond understanding.

Blessed assurance, Jesus is mine!
Oh, what a foretaste of glory divine!
Heir of salvation, purchase of God,
Born of His Spirit, washed in His blood.

This is my story, this is my song,
Praising my Savior all the day long;
This is my story, this is my song,
Praising my Savior all the day long.

> *Perfect submission, perfect delight,*
> *Visions of rapture now burst on my sight;*
> *Angels, descending, bring from above*
> *Echoes of mercy, whispers of love.*
>
> *Perfect submission, all is at rest,*
> *I in my Savior am happy and blest,*
> *Watching and waiting, looking above,*
> *Filled with His goodness, lost in His love.*

Tears trickled down her cheeks, as they often did. Only this time the tears were evidence of the joy she felt. Will walked in the bedroom and hurried to her side when he saw her face.

"Sadie, Honey, what's wrong?" he asked with concern.

"Nothing is wrong. I promise. I just feel … so … blessed. I lay here all day long, and so much of the time I feel sorry for my lot in life. But today I have realized how blessed I am. I have you and my beautiful girls. Kelly has finally turned to the Lord, and He is working all things together for her good and His glory. How many prayers I prayed, Will. And God answered every one. I want to shout it to the world, Will. I feel … well, I guess you would say called. I feel called to something. Which is really quite funny considering I can't even walk," she said with a peaceful smile. "I really would like to talk to Pastor Tom about this. Could you call him for me?"

"Of course, I will." And he got up straight away to do so, not wanting to waste a moment of Sadie's newfound joy.

Four weeks later, Will and Sadie sat in an empty sanctuary.

They had arrived at the church well before anyone else. They needed time to prepare before the rest of the congregation arrived. *What am I doing?* Sadie thought nervously. Will knew what she was thinking by the look on her face.

"You are going to do great, Sadie. I know it. You know these people and love them. And they love you. Just speak from your heart."

Sadie simply nodded, though she did not look reassured.

"Are you ready to get settled?" he asked.

She simply nodded again. He lifted her from her wheelchair, and then placed her gently on the cushion of the front row pew. He then rolled her wheelchair to the stairs of the raised level of the sanctuary and backed it up to the stairs. He pulled the wheelchair up the steps and placed it in front of the altar. Sadie watched as Will lined it up just right, careful to lock the wheels so it wouldn't roll. As she watched him, her heart swelled with love and appreciation. Their life was certainly not what they had imagined when they first married. So many of their plans and dreams had to be laid aside. But that love—that intimate bond—had been forged through the fires of their present reality and she was certain nothing could separate them. As she continued to watch him place a simple music stand in front of the chair and lower it to the height of her wheelchair, she reminisced about the day of their wedding, in this very church. She was scared then, too. But they had vowed to stay together in sickness and in health, til death do us part, and they had. So, today, with Will by her side, she knew she could share her simple story of faith.

After Will got everything set, he came back down the steps toward Sadie. He smiled at her as he lifted her up, much like he had on the night of their wedding so long ago. He spoke gentle words of reassurance as he placed her in the wheelchair and organized her notes on the music stand. Then he pulled up a folding chair right beside her so she wouldn't feel awkward and alone as the parishioners trickled in. Together they nodded and waved to the members of their church family. As the service began with a hymn they sang loudly together, and the words and the sound of Will's voice mingled with hers gave her the confidence she needed to say what God had placed on her heart. After the hymn Will gave her a reassuring squeeze and went to sit off to the side. It was time for Sadie to shine alone.

After Pastor Tom introduced her, she cleared her voice and spoke with barely a tremor.

"I want to share with you this morning what prayer has meant in my life. When I was asked to come before you, about a month ago, I agreed. Then, as I thought more, I hesitated and questioned if I should or if I could. I have never been one to give a witness or a testimony—I've always tried to have my actions be my witness. Somehow, this time I felt that wasn't enough. I really felt the Lord would smile upon me, if I would take this opportunity to tell you just how great prayer has been in my life, and how much it has meant to me.

Prayer has always been a very important and meaningful part of my life. I was very fortunate in being born into a family of strong Christian faith and prayer. I know now, what a friend of mine meant in a letter I received from her shortly after my mother died. She told me although I had lost Mother, how lucky I was to have been blessed with such a rich heritage."

"At the time, I really wondered exactly what she meant in her letter by the word 'heritage'. As I have had a little time, ten years to be exact, to reflect on this, I have grown to understand what she meant. What a great heritage it is to be born into a family who puts prayer first and foremost in their lives; where Christian beliefs and values are not only taught but lived out to the fullest daily. For that part of my being I am truly thankful.

To me, prayer is communication with God. It is a natural expression of our religious nature. We have an inborn consciousness of the reality of God. And instinctively, we share the need of His friendship and feel our helplessness without Him. Therefore, we turn to Him——as the flowers in springtime turn to the sun, as the rivers in their course seek the sea. As St. Augustine has said, 'thou hast made us for Thyself, O God, and our spirits cannot rest until they rest in Thee.' Prayer is the very center of life."

"So, you might say, 'But how has prayer made a difference in your life?' I want to attempt to tell you just that today. Prayer has made all of the difference in my life. It has made the difference as to whether I have been weak or strong. It has made the difference in whether I have accepted or rejected things in my life that I would have preferred to change. And it has made the difference in how I have accepted those things. One of my favorite prayers is the Serenity Prayer which says:

Lord, grant me the serenity to accept the things
I cannot change
The courage to change the things I can
And the wisdom to know the difference.

I have had some hard times in my life just as I'm sure all of you have had or will have at some time. Through these times, I feel I have grown stronger in my prayer life. I feel this has come about because during these times I have been more totally dependent upon God to supply my needs. In these times when my needs have been the greatest so has God been the greatest. I know no matter what may come my way, if I keep this prayer channel open with the Lord, I will be fine. He will supply my needs—maybe not as I see them, but they will be supplied. I would like to share another of my favorite prayers with you at this time.

> *I asked God for strength, that I might achieve,*
> *I was made weak, that I might learn humbly to obey.*
> *I asked for health, that I might do greater things,*
> *I was given infirmity that I might do better things.*
> *I asked for riches, that I might be happy,*
> *I was given poverty that I might be wise.*
> *I asked for power, that I might have the praise of men.*
> *I was given weakness, that I might feel the need of God.*
> *I asked for all things that I might enjoy life.*
> *I was given life, that I might enjoy all things.*
> *I got nothing that I asked for—but everything*
> *I had hoped for.*
> *Almost despite myself, my prayers were answered.*
> *I am, among all men, most richly blessed."*

"The origin of this prayer is unknown, but it is believed to have been written by a soldier at war. And so as I worship, work, and pray with you at this church, I continually desire that my course with God and with other people shall be controlled and strengthened at every point by God Himself. I feel close to God in my heart and in my soul and I shall strive to be directed by God and His Spirit in my prayer life and in my life with others. It is through daily communion with God that our motives are kept pure, our faith strong, and our wills kept in harmony with God's will. So, now let us pray."

Member after member came up the steps to greet Sadie and tell her how inspiring she was. She didn't know about that, but what she did know was that her heart was full, and she was very content. As Will carried her back down the steps after everyone had left the sanctuary, a verse from Psalm 73 she had learned years before came suddenly to her mind, as if the Spirit of God was whispering in her ear. *My flesh and my heart may fail, but God is the strength of my heart and my portion forever.*

Yes, Lord, you are, she thought with a smile.

CHAPTER

24

Kelly washed the few dishes in the sink—remnants of their dinner. She had fixed Stan's favorite dish to celebrate their third anniversary. As the warm, soapy water washed over the dishes as well as her hands, her mind traveled back to the day they said "I do." Once they determined to get married, they did not waste time in planning the wedding. Six months and six days after Stan proposed, Kelly walked down the aisle in her mother's wedding dress. It was a day filled with love, friends, and tradition. One of the highlights was when Will rolled Sadie down the aisle in a wheelchair. They had decorated the chair with white flowers, and Sadie wore a crystal blue dress. They had been unsure if she would be able to attend up until the day of the wedding. But that day she awoke clear-eyed and ready—strengthened by the significance of the day.

Kelly chose to wear her mother's dress for two reasons. One, she knew it would mean so much to Sadie; and if she was unable to attend the ceremony, the dress would symbolize her presence of spirit. Two, the dress symbolized the enduring covenant of marriage. For better, for worse, for richer, for poorer, in sickness and in health, until death do us part. The day Sadie had worn that dress, she had no idea what was ahead. Neither Sadie nor Will knew how each of those vows would be tested in the fires of difficulty and suffering. And yet, keeping those vows through each fiery trial proved to strengthen and purify the love between them.

Kelly longed to have the same enduring love and she had a front row seat watching her parents' love endure and grow with each passing year, in good times and in bad. That is what her wedding day was about. That is what began three years ago. And as is the cycle of life, Kelly and Stan had their own fiery trials to endure.

Kelly turned off the water and grabbed a dish towel to dry her hands as well as the dishes. With only two plates, two forks, and two glasses there was no need to run the dishwasher. As she placed the two plates back on the stack of seldom-used dishes, the reality of the unused plates struck Kelly in the tender, raw place of her heart. They had waited a year before they tried to have a family. At that point Kelly fully expected to immediately plan the décor of the nursery. That is not how it turned out, though. The nursery was still as empty as her womb.

After six months of trying to conceive, Kelly finally made an appointment with her doctor. She had confessed to him about the abortion, but it never occurred to her that she would still endure consequences for that long ago, long forgiven act. And yet, the consequences that followed were severe indeed. She would never forget the day she sat on the cold pleather exam table, dressed only in a paper covering as understanding washed over her like a cold, dirty pail of water. The doctor was kind. He was vague at first, not wanting his diagnosis to bring back the despair and regret he sensed was lurking in the corners of her heart.

"Oh, no. Scarring? From the abortion?" Kelly asked as tears filled her eyes.

"Well, um, scarring can occur in many different ways," he dodged.

But Kelly knew. It was the abortion, which took her first child and continued to steal any future children. And the knowledge of that brought back the nightmares filled with darkness and loud machines and condemnation.

When she was awake and well rested, she could talk herself out of the despair and depression. She carried verses in her pockets and purses—verses that affirmed what she knew to be true. Romans 8:1-3 was one of her favorites and she often spoke it aloud in quiet moments of the day.

"Therefore, there is now no condemnation for those who are in Christ Jesus, because through Christ Jesus the law of the Spirit who gives life has set you free from the law of sin and death. For what the law was powerless to do because it was weakened by the flesh, God did by sending his own Son in the likeness of sinful flesh to be a sin offering," she quoted. She believed this truth in her head, but she struggled for this truth to drop to her heart. *Those twelve inches—from head to heart—is often quite a journey,* her father had frequently said. And as usual, he was right.

Kelly walked to the bathroom and opened the medicine cabinet, retrieving her Clomid. She had faithfully taken the medicine for over a year now, hoping it would help her body conceive. It had not helped.

The next step would begin next week. She would go in for exploratory surgery on Wednesday. She both dreaded and looked forward to the event. Of course, no one wants to undergo surgery, but it was the next step in keeping hope alive. Her arms felt weightless as she lifted them to replace the medicine bottle—weightless and weak. Her empty arms longed to hold a tiny symbol of her love for Stan, and yet, empty they remained. *And it's all my fault,* she thought for the millionth time.

Kelly looked down the deep dark shaft, much like an abandoned elevator shaft. She stood on a tiny ledge and held on for dear life to a metal pole above her head. She craned her neck to look down, but all she saw was the black, dark, endless hole below her. She looked above and saw light at the very top. It was so high up, she felt certain she could not climb to it, and so she stayed frozen in place unable to go up or down. She spent her time looking up and then down, unable to decide which direction she should move.

Suddenly, she heard a tiny cry. *Is it a kitten?* she thought. *No, no it's a baby. A newborn.* But she couldn't see the baby, could barely hear him or her. Certainly, she could not get to the child. Or could she? She made her first attempt at moving from the spot on which she had been cemented. She nearly fell into the dark abyss, but caught hold of the next metal bar just as her right foot lost its footing.

The crying increased and then multiplied. Not just one baby—two or three more had joined in the chorus. *No wait, that's more than three, now it sounds like ten,* she thought as anxiety increased causing adrenaline to flow freely, building her courage to move downward. *I've got to get to the babies,* she thought frantically.

Suddenly, a machine sounded loud and clear, echoing in the shaft. *Oh, no! The elevator! The elevator will crush the babies,* she thought helplessly. And then she paused to listen more closely to the sound growing louder with each passing second. *That's not an elevator,* she thought. *Oh God, help me! I've heard that sound. The roar of my nightmare. The roar of my past. Not again, Lord. I can't go back there. Please help me, God,* she prayed aloud as tears of despair ran freely down her cheeks.

Kelly. Kelly, can you hear me? The faintest whisper coming from the bright light above. *Kelly. I'm here. Can you hear me?*

Yes! Yes! Here I am! Help us! Please help us! she shouted, looking up. As she continued to look up, the light grew brighter and the sound of babies and machines grew fainter, and was replaced by a continuous beep, beep, beep in perfect rhythm.

"Kelly, it's me, Stan. Wake up, Honey." She squinted at the bright light of the recovery room. Stan sat in a chair beside her hospital bed, holding her hand. He smiled her way as she opened her eyes. But despite his smile, she could see it in his eyes. She knew even before he spoke the truth aloud.

"I can't have babies, can I?" she said, more as a statement than a question.

Stan's smile faded, and tears formed as puddles in his blue eyes. He squeezed her hand tightly, and shook his head slowly. "It's very unlikely that you can get pregnant. The doctor said the scarring has closed your fallopian tubes. There is less than a five percent chance we can get pregnant on our own." Kelly looked silently at the bright lights above her bed. In her imagination, she could still hear the faint sound of a baby's cry from her dream. After a moment, she looked at Stan's handsome face, etched with pain and concern. *I will not fall apart. I can't do that to Stan*, she thought with new resolve.

She looked at him and smiled a slight smile that didn't reach her sad eyes. She squeezed his hand and asked, "Okay. What's next?"

"What's next?" involved frequent trips to a fertility specialist in Jackson. The doctor was nice enough, but cautious. He had learned over the years not to give out false hope, and in Kelly's case, there would be very little hope that could not be labeled as false. But he had seen worse cases with positive results, so he laid out a clear, concise plan, making sure they understood all of the facts—simply facts without feelings. And so, they proceeded forward into the uncertain and financially draining world of in vitro fertilization.

This process brought even more heartache for Kelly and Stan. They harvested a whopping 49 eggs and nineteen healthy embryos formed. Stan was terrified they would become pregnant with so many babies they would end up in a prime time documentary with Kelly's grossly disfigured body on display for the world to see. Kelly often thought of her dream and the multiple babies in the dark shaft and she prayed and willed them to come forth.

In time, they lost embryo after embryo, heaping pain upon pain. Kelly and Stan both turned to the Lord for help and healing during this difficult time, though in very different ways. Stan prayed for the strength to accept whatever lot the Lord had determined for their lives. Kelly was not ready for acceptance. She stormed the gates of heaven pouring out her requests like a good soldier in a holy war. It was in this stance of militaristic prayer that she happened upon a verse in her daily Bible reading. Isaiah 61:7.

"Instead of your shame you will receive a double portion, and instead of disgrace you will rejoice in your inheritance. And so you will inherit a double portion in your land, and everlasting joy will be yours," she spoke the holy words aloud each day. *Yes, Lord. May it be so—and soon!* she thought, hope rising in her heart like a beautiful sunrise on a clear, cool morning. *A double portion. That is what I want, Lord. Please, God, give me twins!*

CHAPTER

Will opened the heavy door to Sadie's room. It had been over three years since Sadie had been living in the Assisted Living section of Traceway Manor. Will still felt a twinge of guilt each time he entered the building. They had managed on their own for fifteen years before Sadie's diseased body had taken away her ability to live at home. He had tried for so long to manage it all. But as the girls had grown up and moved out, he found himself unable to both work and care for Sadie at the same time. Sadie needed care around the clock—and not just sitters. Her health had declined so much she needed constant medical care.

Will felt his heart beat faster as a terrible memory came unbidden to the forefront of his mind. For years he simply called it The Day. He had spent years running from The Day, had avoided it as long as he could. It was the day when the inevitable arrived. The day when he had to tell Sadie she must move away from the home she loved, the home they had built together with love, determination and perseverance.

Others may equate home with furniture or paint colors or paintings on the wall. Though Sadie would have loved to be a homemaker in that sense, her body did not allow it. Nor would it allow her to fill her home with sweet scents of favorite recipes or fresh flowers lovingly cared for in her garden. No, all of those images of home were not to be for Sadie. But home represented family, and laughter, and independence to a certain degree. Home was familiar. She was surrounded by memories of better days, and warm conversations, and the hustle and bustle of life.

When Kelly first moved back to Tupelo, after she and Stan were engaged, she lived at home for a time. It was a time cherished by everyone. The month was October and it didn't take Will much effort now to close his eyes and remember the details of that time. The leaves were changing colors and had begun to fall. The air was crisp. Though he, of course, could not go to football games anymore, he loved to hear the good-natured bantering between Mississippi State and Ole Miss fans during the workday.

When Kelly moved back home, Will felt great relief. He had not realized what a toll Sadie's care had taken on him until he had someone once again to share the load. And while he cherished the days together and the help, this time also confirmed he couldn't do it anymore by himself. Still, he tried not to think about the inevitable day Kelly moved out of his house and into Stan's house, where she belonged. He decided instead to cherish each day as it came.

In early December of that year he got a call from Traceway

Manor. He had put Sadie on the waiting list years prior, knowing that The Day would eventually come. He got the call just as Kelly prepared to meet Stan for the annual Christmas Parade. He felt badly that he could not go with them, not because he desperately wanted that pleasure, but because Reed's Department Store sponsored the event. As an administrative employee, he felt he should be there. And yet, once again, he felt his hands were tied. He could not do everything—and he once again chose Sadie, just as he had done since they were teenagers.

Will hung up the phone and stood silently with head bowed. Kelly walked into the kitchen and saw him before he could recover from the devastating phone call.

"Dad, what's wrong," Kelly asked with concern.

Will knew he couldn't hide this from Kelly, though he had intended to wait until after the parade. *Why spoil their fun?* he thought. And yet, he was fresh out of the energy necessary to hide the truth.

"That was Traceway Manor," he said flatly.

"And?" Kelly asked gently.

"They have a spot for Mom," he said as emotion threatened to overtake him.

"Oh, Dad," Kelly said. She tried to think of something encouraging to say. After all, this is what they had waited on for years. And yet, both felt the heavy weight of this decision. Once Sadie moved to Traceway Manor, she would never move back. Yes, she could visit. Will would see to it that she came home for a visit each week. But she would no longer live at home. She would no longer live with him. The truth of that reality gripped his heart and threatened to squeeze it into a million pieces.

After a moment, Kelly spoke. In broken sentences heavy with emotion, she said, "Dad, I know this is hard. I can't imagine what you are feeling. But …" she paused long enough to take a deep breath. "Dad, she has to go."

Will merely nodded, with head down, trying to hide the tears from Kelly. Neither said anything else, and Kelly walked out the back door to meet Stan for the parade. The jingle bells she had placed on the doorknob rang joyfully as she closed the door, mocking him in his time of despair.

Kelly returned from the parade to find her dad sitting peacefully in the den. Sadie was sleeping soundly, after Will had shared a tray of food with her in bed. She could only eat soft foods now, for the threat of choking was real and could be deadly. She had lost control of some of the muscles in her throat and Will only trusted the kind of food that could slide right down. They ate a lot of Kraft Macaroni and Cheese in the blue box. He always ate what Sadie ate, so she would not feel deprived of better cuisine. However, sometimes on the way home from work, he would go through a drive-through window for some "real" food, though he was careful to eat it in the car before he came in the house. He knew Sadie herself would have loved a good burger, if only she could have managed it. This disease had taken away so much of life's simple pleasures. And it was that truth which helped him make his decision. He couldn't take away the simple pleasure of her home and her bed and the family pictures on the wall. He couldn't take away the simple pleasure of how their house smelled or the familiar sounds of the creaking wood floors.

He couldn't do it. Not now. Not before Christmas.

"How was the parade," he asked pleasantly, trying to avoid the topic at hand.

"It was really fun," Kelly replied. "The route was the same as always, and we stood in the same spot we always did when I was little—right in front of Reed's."

"Did you see any old friends?" he asked.

"Yes, I saw tons of people. Not a lot of friends my age, but lots of your friends," she said, hiding the fact that she was grateful not to see her high school friends. She was so different now, and she didn't relish the reminder of how she once was, who she once was. Thankfully, this was now and God had mercifully spared her a rough walk down memory lane.

Kelly spent fifteen minutes describing as many of the floats and cars and horse-drawn carriages as she could remember. She described the children in their Christmas attire singing carols on a decorated flat bed trailer. She described the display of old cars from the Tupelo Automobile Museum, each adorned with a Christmas wreath on the front grill. She described the high school band playing *Joy to the World*, and the Santa with the lopsided fake beard bringing up the rear of the parade.

As a family, they had learned to observe details so they could bring them back for Sadie and Will to savor. If they couldn't go and do, at least Kelly could let them picture it with her descriptions. After she had exhausted her recollections of the Christmas parade, they both fell into an uncomfortable silence. They knew they had to address the situation of moving Sadie to Traceway, but neither wanted to bring it up.

Finally, Will cleared his voice and said, "I have made my decision."

Kelly looked up expectantly and simply waited for him to continue.

"I can't do it, Kelly," he said with conviction. "I can't do that to your mom right now. Not before Christmas. Not before the wedding. I can't deprive her of those joys, even if she can't participate in either one."

"But, Dad, you need help. What if it takes years for a space to open up? What will you do then?"

"I don't know, Kelly. I have to trust that God will provide. And when the time is right, I trust that He will give me a peace about it. I don't have a peace about it now. I can't do it. Not yet," he finished. And Kelly knew that was the end of the discussion.

She got up and walked to the chair where her dad sat. She kissed the top of his head and then leaned down to hug him. As she did, she whispered in his ear, "I hope Stan and I have what you and Mom have. I hope we love each other with the same depth you and Mom love each other."

"You will, Kelly. I know you will."

Kelly bent down and kissed her dad on the cheek and headed upstairs to her childhood room. Will remained in his chair, head down in prayer. He knew he had made the right decision, but the unknowns of the future threatened to wreck his peace. Rather than succumb to the threat of worry, he took his requests to the only One who knew what the future held. When he lifted his head, his peace had returned and his purpose was clear. He saw the Christmas tree in the corner—a real one though artificial would have been easier. Sadie had insisted the smell of the pine was an important part of the holiday. Then he glanced once again at the jingle bells on the doorknob, placed there at Sadie's insistence. She claimed the jingle of the bells signaled the sounds of the season. And he looked at the Nativity scene placed prominently as a focal point of the mantel. Sadie had directed him to place it there, as a reminder that Christ was the reason for the season. *Yes,* he thought to himself, *Sadie has left her mark on this home. Even if she can't do it, she can direct it.*

He rose suddenly from his chair, and walked over to the secretary in the corner, retrieving a note card, envelope and pen. He walked to the kitchen table, sat down, and began to write his feelings to his precious Sadie.

> *Dear Sadie,*
> *I want you to know how much I appreciate everything you do to make Christmas special. All the traditions and how much our girls enjoy Christmas can be credited to you. Thanks for always making Christmas such a special time! I hope and pray the coming year will be filled with peace, joy, and good health for you.*
> *All my love always!*
> *Merry Christmas!*
> *Will*

When he finished writing, he sealed the envelope and tucked it back in the secretary until Christmas morning. He was happy they could share the season in the home they had created together for at least one more year.

Back in the present, Will sat by Sadie's bed in the faux

leather blue chair, which had become his nightly station. After work, Will would grab some dinner—usually take-out or the typical brown-bag sandwich and chips, and head over to visit Sadie. He sat in the blue chair and they talked about his day and then watched their favorite television shows. Of course, only her family and closest caretakers could really understand her anymore. It was much like when the girls were toddlers. Sadie of course could understand them, with their baby pronunciations. She could tell what they were saying just by seeing their expressions. And sadly, now the roles were reversed. Had her girls felt the frustration she felt when her brain said one thing and her tongue said another?

Sadie never wanted to talk about her day. It seemed if she described her day, it made her all the more melancholy. She chose instead to envision the world outside the grey concrete walls and tiled floors of the room in which she lived each hour of the day. Will constantly checked in with the nurses about her physical, mental, and emotional state, and he was constantly assured that Sadie was doing well. She smiled her crooked smile whenever anyone entered the room, and patiently endured the sponge baths, blood pressure checks, and bed sore inspections. She was a sweet and patient resident and was beloved by the whole staff. But when Will was there, she only wanted to talk of home and the outside world. He knew it was because she lived vicariously through his descriptions of a normal life. The knowledge of how she longed to live a normal life was often more than his emotions could take.

He held her hand as they watched a new episode of *Gilmore Girls*, Sadie's choice of course. Though his eyes were on the screen, for some reason, on this night he was not watching the show, but was instead watching a re-run of his own life, three and a half years ago.

It was March of 2000. Sadie had relished every minute hearing the details of Kelly's upcoming May wedding. It seemed surreal that not only was Kelly marrying such a wonderful man, she was also settling down in Tupelo, only a few streets over from her parents. Kelly still lived at home in the days leading up to the wedding, and each day she settled in the chair by the bed and told her mother every detail of the wedding plans, as well as all of her hopes and dreams for the future. *Those were bittersweet days*, Will acknowledged in the silence of his thoughts.

In some ways they were the most precious months since all of the girls left home. But, at the same time, they were the most difficult they had endured. Sadie seemed to change at a rapid pace during those months. While her spirit soared with the added activity at home, her body declined. She lost many of the precious marks of independence, most of which also took away more and more of her dignity. In addition to lost milestones, Sadie also began to have more frequent bouts of choking, one of which resulted in a 911 call.

Just as before, the anticipated phone call came, this time just four months after the first call. As the administrator of Traceway Manor spoke, Will felt his heart break at the thought of Sadie moving away from their shared home. And yet, this time he knew he must proceed.

The night he told Sadie of his decision was one of the hardest of his life. The anguished cries were even harder to bear because her weakened throat muscles turned the cries into a sound more akin to a wounded animal than his sweet, beloved Sadie.

She kept saying over and over between guttural cries, "But I'm only fifty years old. I can't go to a nursing home. I'm only fifty."

In his mind's eye, Will could see himself standing before Sadie's wheelchair, weeping. "Sadie, I just don't know what to do. I cannot do this anymore," he said between sobs.

Seeing Will's heartache stopped Sadie's tears like a faucet turned to curb the flow of water. Quietly she said, "Okay. I'll go." Will looked in her eyes and neither said a word. Then, even more quietly she said with the tiniest bit of hope, "I'll go for six months for a rest period for you." It was almost a question rather than a statement.

"No, Honey. I can't lie to you. It won't do you any good to have a false sense of hope. We have to do this. And it has to be permanent," Will said with conviction, though his heart longed to lie just to curb the immediate pain.

Once again, Sadie began to release deep guttural cries. "I'm only fifty," she said once again. Kelly had been standing across the room, tears streaming down her face, watching the fragile world of her parents break into pieces.

She calmly but quickly walked over to her parents and stood between them. She then kneeled in front of her mother's wheel chair. "Mom," she said in a firm voice, though it broke her heart further to speak the words she knew she must say.

"Look at me, Mom." She waited until Sadie raised her head bowed in grief and pain. Kelly looked into her mother's beautiful blue eyes and said the painful words she had to say. "Mom, you have to do this. Please do it. I am afraid for both of you if you don't."

With tears streaming down her cheeks, Sadie simply nodded her consent, knowing that The Day had sadly arrived.

When the show was over, Will rose from the blue chair and leaned down to kiss his beloved bride. He looked deep in her silver blue eyes and said, "I love you, Sadie. I'll see you tomorrow." Just as he would say every night for the rest of her life.

CHAPTER

26

Kelly stood before the heavy gray door to her mother's room. She paused just a moment before she entered, just as she always did. When they moved her mom to Traceway Manor, it was one of the worst days of her life. On that day, she looked her mom in her eyes and promised her she would not be abandoned. Kelly had kept that promise and every other day for the past four years she had visited with her mother.

You would think I would be used to it by now, Kelly thought to herself. But each trip was hard. Each visit started with a pause before the heavy gray door, praying for strength for her mom as well as herself. Kelly hated to see Sadie in this setting. The heavy gray door stood as a reminder of the heavy gray life her mother led each day. And just like she must gather strength to push through the door to Sadie's room, Kelly was determined to push through the heaviness of the situation.

Today will be easier than most days, Kelly thought as she pasted a smile on her face. *Mom's going to be so excited!* She pushed through the doorway and saw her mother sleeping in the hospital bed across the room. She guided the door closed so it would not wake up Sadie, then quietly picked up a chair and moved it beside the bed.

Kelly sat down and looked at her mom, noticing her head had fallen at an odd angle, her mouth was slightly ajar, and her breathing was labored with the effort it took to take a breath. Kelly noticed for the first time how smooth her mother's skin was—so soft and smooth and glowing. Despite the hardships Sadie faced on a daily basis, there were elements of beauty this disease had not stolen. Sadie's crystal blue eyes and her glowing, smooth, wrinkle-free skin had always been her best features. And they still were. *She looks too young to be a grandmother*, Kelly thought with a smile, and suddenly felt she couldn't wait another moment to share the good news.

"Mama? Mama, can you hear me? It's me, Kelly," she said gently as she took Sadie's soft hand in hers. Sadie slowly opened her blue eyes, though it took a few moments of prodding for Kelly to really get her attention. This seemed to happen more and more often. Most of the time, Sadie followed conversation with her eyes and knew exactly what was being said, even if she was sometimes too tired to respond with garbled words, which had become her own unique language. But lately, every now and then, the effort to pay attention seemed swallowed up by the fatigue she felt most of the day. It helped when they could get her in her wheelchair and roll her outside on the patio. There they could gather around the picnic tables and act, if only for a few minutes, like a real family. Sadie loved those days, though they seemed to take such a toll on her, they were saved for special occasions. Today is a special occasion, Kelly thought and thus said, "Mom? Would you like to go outside today?"

It took the effort of two nurses plus Kelly to get her mom

into the wheelchair, out of the room, and onto the patio. It was a beautiful spring day with a crystal blue sky and only occasional puffy white clouds floating lazily across. Sadie strained to lift her head up to the sky and seemed to breathe deeply, taking in the freshness of the air. Kelly pushed her down the wide entrance walkway and made a sharp left through a gate, entering a fenced-in courtyard. In the courtyard Sadie and family enjoyed brief, beautiful moments together and during those times, Sadie could pretend they were a normal family, gathering together on a normal sunny day.

Kelly pushed the wheelchair to the picnic table in the back left corner of the courtyard. This was their family spot. The brief shared memories at that table were like a magnet, and Kelly would not settle for another spot. When Sadie's wheelchair was secure, Kelly sat at the table close to Sadie and took a deep breath, soaking in the fresh air and the fragrance of the blooming bushes in the beds near by. She was suddenly grateful for this spot. It was not what any of them would have chosen, but it was clean and well-cared for, and some precious soul made sure the residents and families had a spot filled with beautiful living things. Subconsciously, this encouraged them all to continue to choose to live with purpose, despite their circumstances—"blooming where you are planted" took on a whole other dimension in this place of struggle where Sadie had found herself for the past four years.

"Mom, I have something to tell you," Kelly began, unable to hold back her joy any longer.

Sadie's eyes were clear now, and though her communication skills were lacking, there was nothing wrong with her brain, nor her motherly instinct. Even before Kelly continued, Sadie found herself welling with joyful anticipation.

Kelly took both of her mother's hands in hers and continued, "Mom, you are going to be a grandmother again! And I am going to finally be a mother!"

Sadie's face beamed in full understanding and tears filled the corners of her eyes.

"And Mom," Kelly continued. "Mom, I'm having twins! A double portion, just like I prayed!"

Sadie could not bring forth the words in the recesses of her mind, but there really was no need to express with words what showed clearly in her face. Mother and daughter embraced for a long time, both letting tears flow freely, without the need to wrap the emotion in words.

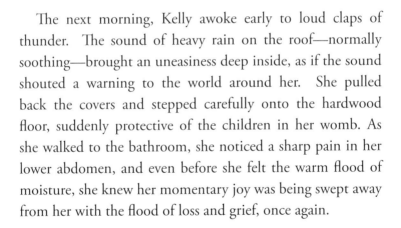

The next morning, Kelly awoke early to loud claps of thunder. The sound of heavy rain on the roof—normally soothing—brought an uneasiness deep inside, as if the sound shouted a warning to the world around her. She pulled back the covers and stepped carefully onto the hardwood floor, suddenly protective of the children in her womb. As she walked to the bathroom, she noticed a sharp pain in her lower abdomen, and even before she felt the warm flood of moisture, she knew her momentary joy was being swept away from her with the flood of loss and grief, once again.

CHAPTER

27

Kelly parked in the closest available space in front of the large red brick building. Parkgate Pregnancy Clinic. The sign was hung among others on the front of the building, indicating in which suite the clinic was located. Suite 2A. *It must be upstairs*, she thought, as she looked up toward the large windows on the second floor. She sat in the car for a few moments, gaining the strength to open the car door and move inside. She and Stan had agreed that doing something for others is the best way to get the focus off yourself. *The Lord knows I have focused on myself enough lately,* she thought. She had grieved for two months now. It was time to move forward. *I can't do anything about the children I have lost, but I can help others not lose theirs.* With that thought, she took a deep breath and opened the car door.

When she entered the reception area, she was greeted with a genuine smile and she immediately felt at ease.

"Hello, there. How can I help you?" the smiling lady asked.

"Hi. I'm Kelly Williams. And I want to volunteer," Kelly replied simply.

"That's great! We always need volunteers. There is an

interview process to go through first, just to make sure you are ready for some of the difficult situations you may encounter as you volunteer. Usually, I would schedule that, but I am all caught up on my paperwork and there are no clients scheduled for another hour, so we could go ahead and do that now, if you would like. My name is Melissa, by the way."

"That would be great," Kelly thought, relieved she would not have to come back to get the process started. She needed to help someone soon. *That's how I will help myself,* she thought.

She followed Melissa toward the back of the building and they entered a large office space, where Melissa motioned toward a set of club chairs by the window. As she settled in the chair, she looked out the window toward the back of the building. "How beautiful," she commented. What she saw was a large garden, beautifully appointed with shrubs and flowers and narrow paths filled with pebbled rock. There was a large bronze statue of Jesus with such a look of tenderness and love, Kelly felt tears sting the corners of her eyes.

"That is our Garden of Hope. You see those wooden boxes along the path?" she paused and pointed until Kelly nodded. "Those are filled with Scriptures—all sorts of God's promises of forgiveness and healing and peace. Our clients often walk through the garden as they go through the healing process."

"How beautiful," Kelly said once again. She couldn't think of another response because her mind was already strolling through the garden in her imagination. *What would it be like to feel truly free of all this grief and pain,* she thought, and once again, tears stung her eyes. She willed them away and smiled at Melissa.

For the next fifteen minutes, Melissa asked Kelly questions from the clipboard in her lap and wrote down her responses. Most of the questions were simple information such name, address, family members, what church she attended, and how she had heard about Parkgate. But she also asked Kelly a simple question with a not-so-simple answer.

"Why do you want to volunteer here, Kelly?"

"Well, I want to help people. I really need to help someone right now," she paused, then added quickly to her own great surprise, "And I've had an abortion."

Melissa paused and quietly placed the clipboard and pen on the table in between the chairs. She scooted up in her chair and took Kelly's hand in hers. With great compassion, she said, "I've had an abortion, too, Kelly. That is also why I want to help the women who come through the doors of this clinic. But trust me on this: You can't help others until you have helped yourself—at least in this type of situation. It is very painful to walk with someone through the decision of whether or not to have an abortion. And if you haven't dealt fully with your own pain, you will drown in the stress of it all." She paused just a moment to gauge Kelly's reaction. The tears that had continuously stung her eyes, now slid down her cheeks. She simply nodded.

Melissa smiled gently with understanding and Kelly knew she could be trusted. "Kelly, I sometimes mentor women one-on-one. We go through a Bible Study called *Surrendering the Secret*. It is an 8 session course by a lady named Pat Layton. She has her own abortion story, too. But she and I both have found freedom from our secrets, our sins—only through the truth found in God's Word. I would love to walk this journey with you, if you think you are ready," She paused, waiting on Kelly to process the information. She didn't have to wait long.

"I'm ready," Kelly said with certainty.

And with that tiny step, Kelly felt joy and peace for the first time in a long while.

CHAPTER

28

The sky was crystal blue as Kelly pulled into the parking lot. The now familiar brick building brought a feeling of comfort. *It had not felt that way at first*, Kelly thought as she got out of the car and walked to the front door.

As she walked up the stairs to Suite 2A, she reflected on the journey she had traveled over the past seven weeks. *It has been hard, that's for sure*, Kelly thought, as she climbed the last few stairs. *I guess that is what I am doing now*, she thought. *Climbing the last few stairs of this journey.* A month ago she almost quit meeting with Melissa, but Stan encouraged her to continue. It had been hard on him, too. He had to endure details of her life which acted as a knife into his heart—details he would have preferred not to have known. But the secrets were all gone now—every one of them. It wasn't just the secrets surrounding the abortion that had been brought into the light of the love of Christ. It was also the haunting secrets of the nightmare she endured at the Alabama farm so many years ago. And with every secret revealed, and its accompanying bondage released, Kelly felt free for the first time since she was six-years-old.

Stan was so loving and supportive, Kelly did not know what she would have done without him. He held her and cried along with her as she ripped open the scars of long ago. Just as a broken bone must sometimes be re-broken for a proper healing, so Kelly's deepest wounds had to be painfully re-visited for her to be healthy and whole.

She opened the door and saw Melissa sitting in the reception area just as she had that first day. She smiled a big smile, greeting her close friend with unspoken words.

"Hey, there," Melissa said. "How are you?"

"I am actually good," Kelly replied honestly.

Melissa smiled with joy and understanding and replied, "I'm so glad! Are you ready for today?"

"Yes, I'm ready," Kelly said.

"Then let's get to work," Melissa replied as she rose from her chair and led Kelly down the bright hall decorated with beautiful photos of children. Kelly dropped her purse in Melissa's office as they passed by and followed her friend out the back door toward the beautiful Garden of Hope.

Kelly and Melissa had spent many hours in the serene space behind the Parkgate office during the past few weeks. The paths through the garden were designed to mirror the journey of the women in crisis pregnancy situations; and together with Melissa, Kelly walked, meditated, and cried through each station. The garden's path was marked with redemptive Bible verses she memorized and continued to savor each day. *I will probably always need to remind myself of the truth in those verses,* she thought. But she knew that over time, the truth had finally fallen from her head to her heart.

Kelly's eyes traveled to the statue in the center of the garden. It was a beautiful bronze statue of Jesus sitting with a mother, cradling her child. That is the spot to which Melissa led Kelly on this beautiful morning. They made their way to the bench perfectly situated to observe the statue and both sat down in comfortable silence. Kelly closed her eyes and felt the cool breeze on her face. *How good of God to give me a beautiful day today,* she thought.

That had not been the case four weeks ago. On that day, there had been dark clouds, pouring rain, and raging thunder. The outside storm didn't even compare to the storm inside Kelly's heart that day. On that day she chose to forgive, and it was a hard-fought battle. Thankfully, she won through God's powerful truth and Melissa's gentle guidance.

On that day, they had observed the garden from the window in Melissa's office. Kelly had sat by the window as she wrote a letter to her abuser, describing the pain, shame, and trauma he had inflicted on her. She poured out her pain, anger, and hatred, surprised at how quickly the words came forth. Her heart felt fury for the loss of innocence and years overshadowed with heartache.

Two hours later, with Melissa by her side, Kelly had walked out the back door to the garden. Though the clouds were still dark and gloomy, the storm was slowly subsiding. They stood together in the drizzle and set the letter on fire. They watched until the fire consumed the paper, and the Holy Spirit consumed the anger and hatred in her heart. Melissa read the scripture from the nearest station along the garden's path. It was Isaiah 43:1-3.

> *But now, this is what the Lord says—*
> *he who created you, Jacob,*
> *he who formed you, Israel:*

> *"Do not fear, for I have redeemed you;*
> *I have summoned you by name; you are mine.*
> *When you pass through the waters,*
> *I will be with you;*
> *and when you pass through the rivers,*
> *they will not sweep over you.*
> *When you walk through the fire,*
> *you will not be burned;*
> *the flames will not set you ablaze.*
> *For I am the Lord your God,*
> *the Holy One of Israel, your Savior;*

Today, the storm had ceased. She had walked through the flood and fire of grief and shame and had not only survived, but thrived. Today was a monumental day, as it was the end of their study and the beginning of the next phase of her healing journey. Today, she would name her child, lost so long ago. She had thought and prayed for days about the appropriate name to give her first-born child. Though she did not know the gender of her child, her heart felt sure it was a boy. She searched her Bible for Biblical names. Though many of the names she found could have aptly applied, she knew she had found the right one, when she came across the story of Hannah. Hannah was another broken woman, wracked with pain. Hannah also had longings and fears and failures. Hannah had turned to God, and God had heard. Hannah also had to surrender her son to the redemptive care of her God.

Melissa handed Kelly a large, smooth stone and a black marker.

"Are you ready?" Melissa asked gently.

"I am," Kelly replied. She then wrote the name of her lost son on the smooth stone. Tears trickled down her cheeks, and Melissa lovingly rubbed her back as she wrote.

"His name is Samuel," Kelly said simply. "His name means 'God has heard'. It seemed to fit. I know God has heard me. He has forgiven me and loves me. Samuel is with God now. One day I will hold him and tell him how much I love him. And how sorry I am." Melissa nodded and smiled as her own tears gently fell. Together, they walked over to the bronze statue and placed the stone with Samuel's name, gently at the feet of Jesus.

CHAPTER

Kelly and Melissa sat comfortably in the chairs in Melissa's office once again. Today, they were not discussing Kelly's situation, but the heartbreaking situation of another young woman. Kelly was two months into her job as a volunteer counselor at Parkgate. They had rejoiced over several babies saved and wept over a few babies lost. Kelly grieved to know the heartache those mothers would endure in the coming years. *But God can redeem it all*, she told them with assurance.

"Kelly, today I have a meeting in New Albany. I wondered if you would have time to take this paperwork by New Beginnings for me."

"Sure, I can," Kelly replied.

New Beginnings was the local adoption agency which often worked alongside Parkgate when a woman chose to implement an adoption plan. New Beginnings was aptly named, as it provided a new beginning for many babies, as well as birth mothers who chose to release their child to a better home and situation. *That's the most loving thing some mothers could ever do for their child*, Kelly thought, as she drove to New Beginnings headquarters on Southridge Drive.

Kelly parked to the side of the stucco building and then walked down the wide covered sidewalk toward the front door. When she entered, she was greeted with a friendly, genuine smile of a brown-haired, blue-eyed young woman at the front desk.

"Hi. Can I help you?"

"Yes, I'm Kelly Williams. I volunteer at Parkgate Pregnancy Clinic. Melissa asked me to drop this paperwork by here."

"Great. Thanks, Kelly. My name is Renea, by the way," she said as she reached for the paperwork.

"Nice to meet you, Renea. How long have you worked at New Beginnings?" Kelly asked

"For a couple of years now. It is very rewarding. I love to see babies connected to their forever homes. And we have the great opportunity to help the birth moms, as well. Many hard situations, but many happy endings," she said with a smile.

Kelly paused for a moment, surprising herself with the question she was about to ask.

"Renea, could you tell me a little bit about the adoption process? You see, my husband and I—Well, I guess I am just curious."

An hour later, Kelly left New Beginnings with a seed of a new beginning planted deep in the soil of her heart.

Kelly and Stan acted quickly once they made the decision. They worked with New Beginnings to complete their Home Study, and prepare the portfolio necessary for a birth mother to get a glimpse into their home and hearts. Kelly worked tirelessly through the endless paperwork and turned it over to

Renea in record time. Kelly and Stan trusted God's timing in the placement of their future adopted child, but Kelly felt an urgency she couldn't quite explain. When her friend, Wendy, spoke of their adoption agency in Indiana, Kelly decided to inquire into the wait time of the GLAD Agency, which stood for Greater Love Adoption Decisions.

The first time Kelly spoke on the phone with Julie Smith she felt an instant connection. Without making a commitment, Julie encouraged Kelly to speak with New Beginnings about sharing the information found in the Home Study and portfolio. New Beginnings gladly agreed. The core foundation of New Beginnings was the belief that every child should be able to experience the security of being in a stable home and the nurture and care of loving parents, and if that child was in Indiana, the quicker the placement the better the situation.

Julie encouraged Kelly to be patient, which was easier said than experienced. Stan calmed her with the truth that God knew the best timing. It had, after all, been only six months since they had lost the twins, although the journey Kelly and Stan had walked during the last six months felt like six years. As her due date for the twins approached, Kelly felt a cloud of grief lingering in the edges of her mind and heart. She pushed the cloud back with the truth of her newfound freedom, and the hope of a future child to hold, nurture, and love. Still, each day she hoped for a call, though a match this soon would be miraculous indeed.

On October 24, Kelly received a phone call from Julie Smith. Her hands shook as she saw the name on the caller ID. *She probably just has a question about the paperwork*, Kelly told herself as she answered the phone.

"Kelly, this is Julie. I know this is sudden, but we actually have a birth mother interested in your file. That doesn't mean she will pick you as the adoptive parents, but she is interested. But before we proceed further, I have some information that you and Stan will have to discuss. The woman is pregnant with twins."

Kelly was silent, tears forming in her eyes, emotion preventing her voice to speak.

"Now this is not something you have to say yes to, Kelly. Twins are not for everyone," Julie quickly replied, hoping to alleviate any false sense of responsibility Kelly may be feeling.

"No, Julie. I understand all of that. But I am beyond certain we are interested in twins," Kelly replied with a shaky voice.

As she hung up the phone, the words of the prophet Isaiah echoed once more in her mind and heart, and she whispered the words aloud as she thanked her God, certain that this was His plan for their family.

"*'Instead of your shame you will receive a double portion, and instead of disgrace you will rejoice in your inheritance. And so you will inherit a double portion in your land, and everlasting joy will be yours.'* Thank-you, Jesus!" she said aloud as she picked up the phone to call Stan and share the happy news.

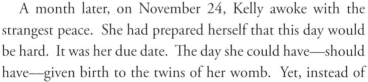

A month later, on November 24, Kelly awoke with the strangest peace. She had prepared herself that this day would be hard. It was her due date. The day she could have—should have—given birth to the twins of her womb. Yet, instead of grief, Kelly felt hope.

The day was cool, the leaves were brilliant colors of red,

yellow, and orange. Thanksgiving was on Thursday, and she knew she had much to be thankful for. She no longer wanted to wallow in the grief, nor let her mind wander to all the what-ifs of her life. She just wanted to be thankful.

When the phone rang later that morning, Kelly was not even surprised when she heard Julie Smith's familiar voice on the other end. She smiled knowingly when she heard the news. They had been selected to become parents of twins—their double portion.

By Christmas Eve they were back home with Bella and Evie, joyfully juggling diapers and formula feedings every three hours. Their hands and hearts were full. In the wee hours of Christmas morning, she held her twins as she lay in bed beside Stan, the love of her life. As she looked around her she felt like shouting *Joy to the World! The Lord has come!* Instead, she quietly sang in the faintest whisper,

Silent night, Holy night
All is calm, all is bright
Round yon virgin, mother and child
Holy infant, tender and mild
Sleep in heavenly peace,
Sleep in heavenly peace.

Silent night, Holy night
Son of God, love's pure light
Radiant beams from thy holy face
With the dawn of redeeming grace,
Jesus, Lord at thy birth
Jesus, Lord at thy birth.

> *Silent night, Holy night*
> *Shepherds quake, at the sight*
> *Glories stream from heaven above*
> *Heavenly, hosts sing Hallelujah.*
> *Christ the Savior is born,*
> *Christ the Savior is born.*

As the final verse escaped from her lips, she closed her eyes and gave thanks to the One born long ago, who came to redeem the world—even her world.

CHAPTER

Fourteen-year-old Tessa hopped off the school bus at the corner of the street where her grandmother lived. She always thought of her house that way—where her grandmother lived—as if she was still just visiting after all these years. Tessa always felt displaced, as if she was perpetually waiting to go home—only she didn't know where home was.

She walked slowly up the driveway, trying to remember if she had done her chores the night before, and wondering what reaction her grandmother would have if she hadn't. The word "unpredictable" described her relationship with her grandmother. There were times of laughter and peace. She knew her grandmother loved her deep down. *Surely she does,* Tessa often thought. *She wouldn't have taken me in if she didn't love me … Would she?*

The gnawing thought which remained in the recesses of her mind was that she was truly all alone and unlovable. She would not have voiced that thought aloud to anyone, but she felt it, most every day. Little did she know how much that thought dictated her actions.

She was a people-pleaser. She tried to please her

grandmother by staying on top of the growing number of chores required of her. As her grandmother's health slowly declined, so Tessa's responsibilities at home increased. She tried to please her friends. She was willing to do anything and everything they asked of her, even if it meant she might get in trouble at school. Lately, she found herself trying to please the boys who constantly flocked around her, drawn to her bright beautiful hazel eyes, her long, thick dark hair and her beautiful smile which constantly hid the state of her heart, mind, and emotions.

She climbed the creaking steps of the porch, and as she drew near to the screen door, she heard multiple voices. Though she didn't recognize the voices, something felt uneasy. The feeling quickly grew with each step, so much so she would have fled the sound if she had any other place to run. Without another option, she pressed forward toward the unknown voices.

Her eyes adjusted to the darkness of the room. Lights were rarely turned on in an effort to save on the electric bill. But the darkness suited Tessa as it matched the darkness she felt deep inside. She looked toward the green recliner where her grandmother always sat, hoping the familiar face would stop her heart from racing. It did not. She then looked toward the couch just as her grandmother said in an overly cheerful voice, "Why, Tessa, look who's here!"

It only took a glance to remember who sat before her. It was her mother, Roy, and Silvia. They had changed plenty—their lifestyle had obliviously taken a toll. But Tessa would never have forgotten their eyes. In the space of a millisecond, several waves of emotion swept over Tessa, causing her to lose her balance, just like the ocean waves did the one time she went to the beach with her grandmother. She remembered that trip well—all the sand, water, and fun. But what stood out most of all was the panic she felt when a wave knocked her feet out from under her and the tide kept her underwater for what seemed like an eternity. When she was finally free from the grip of the wave, all she could do was stagger to the beach and sit on the sand, gasping for breath. And that is exactly what she did now. She staggered over to the other chair across the room, and sat down roughly before she lost her footing once again.

"Well, Tessa, say hello to your mother and her friends. I've taught you better than to act so rude," her grandmother said, the cheerfulness now covered with an edge of irritation.

"Hello," Tessa obediently replied.

Tammy was the first to speak. Her words were shaky, as if she were extremely nervous—or needed another fix, which was very likely. "Hi, Tessa. You have changed so much. I can't believe how much you have grown," her mother said, as if the passing years and their subsequent changes were all Tessa's fault—as if she chose to stay hidden from her mother, when in reality she longed to be held by her.

Both Roy and Silvia smiled at Tessa, but Roy's gaze lingered far longer than Silvia's. And the glint in his eyes caused Tessa to pick up the backpack she had placed on the floor by her chair and hold it tightly against her chest, as if it would somehow protect her from whatever he was thinking.

"Tessa, your mom wants to know if you want to go stay with her for a while, now that you are older," her grandmother said bluntly.

Tessa stared at her grandmother, wondering if she had heard her correctly. A tiny bit of hope began to take root in her heart as she sat trying to think of a response. *My mother wants me?* she thought incredulously. A tiny smile formed at the corner of her mouth, but before the smile reached her eyes, she looked back toward the couch and saw Roy's face—as if he were hungry for something—something Tessa had. And then she knew. There was evil motive behind the request. She didn't know whether her mother's motive was one of love, but she knew that Roy's motive was not. And Roy controlled everything in her mother's world. In the space of a few seconds, Tessa had her answer.

"I don't think so," Tessa replied flatly. She then stood up and resolutely grabbed her backpack, and walked back through the screened door. She didn't have any place to go, so she just walked back down the road, away from the house, away from her mom, away from the evil she knew waited for her if she went back to the trailer at the bottom of the steep gravel driveway.

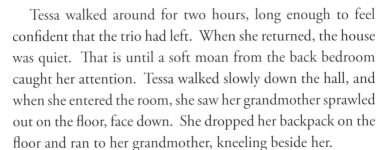

Tessa walked around for two hours, long enough to feel confident that the trio had left. When she returned, the house was quiet. That is until a soft moan from the back bedroom caught her attention. Tessa walked slowly down the hall, and when she entered the room, she saw her grandmother sprawled out on the floor, face down. She dropped her backpack on the floor and ran to her grandmother, kneeling beside her.

"Grandma! Are you okay? Did he hurt you?" she asked as she turned her grandmother on her side. She moaned at the motion, obviously in pain, though not enough pain to prevent the edge of irritation to once again override her voice.

"Who are you talking about? Roy? Of course he didn't

hurt me, child. Are you crazy? I just fell that's all. My blood pressure must have gotten low. Help me up."

Tessa slid her arms under her grandmother's arms and pulled her up from the back. She struggled with the dead weight, thankful the fall had taken place right beside the bed. Both she and her grandmother fell on the bed, and Tessa carefully slid out from under her. She helped her grandmother under the covers and brought her a glass of water. Throughout the evening, Tessa carefully took care of her grandmother—checking on her and taking her a tray of food for dinner. When Tessa finally lay down in her bed late that night, the fear and trauma of seeing her mom, Roy, and Silvia had begun to subside. And the calming thought Tessa had as she drifted off to sleep was this: *Grandma will not make me go away now. She needs me too much.*

And though she would never have admitted it to Tessa, the same thought was heavy on her grandmother's mind as she too drifted off to sleep that night.

CHAPTER

31

Tessa lay in her twin bed, listening to the sound of her grandmother's soft snoring in the next room. The thin walls were no match for the sound, and it was comforting and irritating all at once. Her grandmother had mellowed over the past two years, ever since the night of her fall. She seemed resigned to the fact that she needed Tessa to take care of her, which was all right with Tessa for she needed to be needed. And at least it provided a bit of insurance for a place to lay her head at night. Tessa was now responsible for all the grocery shopping which brought the added perk of having free reign of her grandmother's car. It was a 1985 two-toned Chevy Impala. No beauty, but fairly reliable to get her where she wanted to go.

She was having trouble falling asleep, not only because of her grandmother's snoring, but also because of the troubling scenes she kept reliving in her mind. She had definitely been through worse, so she wasn't even sure why their words hurt so badly. *Sticks and stones and all that*, she thought, though the childhood poem didn't take away the sting.

It had all started in math class. She had befriended a new

girl in town, the new Methodist pastor's daughter. The girl's name was Wendy, and she knew no one at the high school. Tessa certainly understood what it was like to feel like an outsider, plus Wendy knew nothing of Tessa's background, which felt like a safer place to start a friendship. So, Tessa reached out to her in an atypical act of friendliness. After a couple of weeks of chatting in class, Wendy invited Tessa to Wednesday night church. Church attendance was not something Tessa had ever considered, but she was so glad to be asked, she readily accepted. *I bet she wouldn't have asked me if she knew my background*, she thought, glad they were still on level ground.

She sat by Wendy during the pot luck supper, enjoying the community as well as the homemade chocolate pie. *Almost feels like a family*, she thought, as the warmth of the environment spread a peaceful feeling over her. *I will definitely come back.*

She sat quietly during the service and tried to listen, although she didn't really understand the point of the pastor's message. *I guess I would have had to attend Sunday School to understand what he is talking about*, she thought. The whole experience reminded her of going to church long ago with her friend, Mary. *The weekend my mom left me*, she thought as a cold chill replaced the peaceful feeling she had enjoyed. Still, she was determined to put the past behind her and going to church was a good first step. She left the church with a peaceful, light feeling and promised Wendy she would come back next week.

The good feeling lasted well into the next day, up until lunch time. Tessa was in the bathroom when she heard a group of laughing girls enter. She peeked out of the stall door and saw some of the same girls who had also attended the church service.

"Did y'all see Tessa Thomas at church last night?" one of the girls asked, her voice filled with the sing-song melody of gossip.

"Yeah," another replied. "I bet she just came for the free food." And all of the group responded with laughter.

Tessa backed away from the door of the stall, suddenly overcome with the hot and cold reaction of embarrassment, hurt, and shame. She stayed cowered in the stall until every last one of them left the bathroom. She remained there for several minutes after they left, wanting to make certain none of them knew she had been in there.

She lay in her twin bed that night rehashing the scene over and over again, imagining different scenarios, conversations and come-backs. And with each scenario she envisioned, her heart grew harder, her soul more protected. *One thing is for sure*, she thought with determination, *I will never go back to church.*

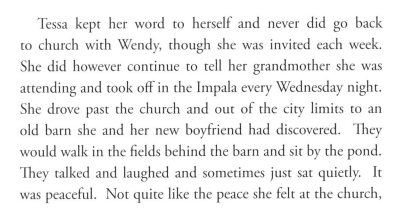

Tessa kept her word to herself and never did go back to church with Wendy, though she was invited each week. She did however continue to tell her grandmother she was attending and took off in the Impala every Wednesday night. She drove past the church and out of the city limits to an old barn she and her new boyfriend had discovered. They would walk in the fields behind the barn and sit by the pond. They talked and laughed and sometimes just sat quietly. It was peaceful. Not quite like the peace she felt at the church, but she would take what she could get. After many weeks, the peace turned to passion and the Wednesday night routine became a rendezvous. The repercussions of those Wednesday nights would change the course of her life in ways she could never have imagined.

CHAPTER

32

"Pregnant? What do you mean you're pregnant?" Grandma screamed with such force, Tessa cowered back into the corner of the sofa. Grandma quickly came within inches of her face screaming all the words about her character Tessa had screamed in her own mind. *It's all true,* Tessa thought. She agreed with every adjective her grandmother called her. The only thing she didn't agree with was what to do next.

"Get rid of it. Immediately," Grandma said with finality. "I can't afford to feed another mouth. You are not fit to be a mother. There is no other option. Get rid of it. I will loan you the money but you will have to pay me back," she concluded, her voice slightly more compassionate.

"I am not going to get rid of it, Grandma. I'm going to have this baby. It didn't do anything wrong; I did. It doesn't deserve to die," Tessa paused leaving her thoughts unspoken. *I do,* she thought with self-loathing.

"If you won't get rid of it, then you're not staying here," Grandma said as she fled to the calm of her bedroom and slammed the door with a force that caused Tessa to jump.

Even with the terrible option before her, Tessa could not abort her baby. She lay in her bed that night, tears streaming down her face. She held up her arms toward the sky and said aloud in a voice just above a whisper, "God, if you are really there, I need help. I know I don't deserve Your help, but I really need it. I have made a mess of an already terrible life. I don't want to mess up the life of my baby, and I know I will. But I don't think killing it is the answer. I don't have any where to go and I don't know what to do. Please help me."

She turned over and sobbed into her pillow, not wanting to give her grandmother the satisfaction of hearing her miserable cries through the thin walls of the house. When she finally calmed down and the lure of sleep came slowly upon her, one word formed clearly in her mind, bringing just enough peace and comfort to allow her to drift off to sleep filled with troubled dreams. It was the word *adoption*.

CHAPTER

33

Kelly pulled off the county road onto the long gravel driveway of her home. She and Stan had built the house on family land, determined to give the twins a delightful fresh-aired childhood. *I just didn't realize what that longer drive would demand*, she thought as she turned off ignition of the van and parked in the garage. Even with the long drive from town, Kelly loved her country home. It was so peaceful, so quiet. *Almost too quiet when the twins are at preschool*, she thought. She grabbed two bags of groceries in the backseat and balanced them on her knee while she looked for her keys in her purse. She stumbled into the house just before she dropped the groceries onto the floor of the mud room. An hour later she had put away the groceries, cleaned the kitchen, made the beds, folded a load of clothes from the dryer and started another load in the washing machine. As she walked down the upstairs hallway to put away the folded clothes, she paused at the door of the huge upstairs playroom. Even with all the toys scattered about, the room seemed empty.

They weren't even supposed to have this room. This was drawn up in the plans as a future option, but with unclear communication between the builder and contractor, they came home one day during the building process to find it fitted with sheetrock and ready to be painted. With that turn of events, they decided to go ahead and finish out the space as they built their home. Sometimes Kelly felt guilty for all the space, knowing it was more than four people needed.

There was something about seeing the room on this day, with laundry basket in hand, which filled Kelly with a great, surprising desire. *I want to fill it up—I want to fill up this house with more children who need a good, loving home,* she thought with certainty. *Now, how I am I going to tell Stan?* she wondered as she returned to her chores.

The seed of desire planted on that day continued to grow with great speed and intensity. She found the courage to tell Stan who approached the subject just as he always did—with caution and wisdom.

"Kelly, we need to pray about this first. We don't need to bust ahead of God. We need to seek His plans—and our bank accounts. Remember, another adoption will be a big expense we haven't planned for."

"I know, Stan. But promise me you will pray about it. Could I at least call Renea at New Beginnings and inquire if they could use our old Home Study? Just in case we decide yes?" she asked, trying hard to keep a begging tone at bay.

As Stan went about seeking God in his way, Kelly sought Him in hers. And that included storming the gates of heaven.

"Lord, send us more children. I will take any child you want to give me. Make it happen, Lord," she prayed in earnest as she knelt by the couch each morning during her quiet time. As time had passed, her desires had become very clear. She wanted another child—believed she was called to adopt another child. And she wanted a son.

One stormy day she knelt by the couch and prayed for a son once again. As soon as she knelt, words came unbidden to her mind—words of condemnation, which she had thought were long since silenced. *"You had a son, and you lost him. You keep asking for a son; I gave you one. Do you think I will give you another?"* The words in her mind cut her heart and she almost rose from her knees, fleeing the reproach of God. But before she could get up off the floor another group of words came to her mind, this time in the recognizable voice of her good Shepherd, her gentle Savior. *"Therefore, there is now no condemnation for those who are in Christ Jesus."*

"Is that You, Lord?" Kelly prayed. "Surely the other words were not from You. It must have been the enemy of my soul—or at least my own feeble flesh still trying to make sense of what will never make sense. But You have told me in Your Word that Your sheep recognize the voice of the Shepherd. And I am one of Yours, Lord. I will only listen to Your Voice."

On that day, Kelly decided to begin a prayer fast. She had participated in a time of fasting in days past. There was something powerful about depriving herself of what she wanted in order to seek God in what she needed. This time, she felt her fast would not be one day or three days or even a week. But on this day, she felt led to an indefinite time of fasting. She decided to fast all things sweet, which was quite the sacrifice given her insatiable sweet tooth.

"That's it, Lord. That's what I will do. I won't eat sweets until You bring me my sweet son."

Two months later, Kelly had finished all the updating necessary to bring their Home Study under compliance of the adoption laws in Mississippi. She knew they would have a long wait ahead of them, but she was relieved to know she had done what she could do right now, which put them one step closer to their child. Three weeks after she submitted the last piece of paperwork, Renea from New Beginnings called. Kelly tried to remain calm when she realized who was on the other end of the phone call.

"Kelly, I wanted to tell you about a young girl who is living in our group home for birth moms. She is sixteen years old and seven months pregnant with a baby boy. She called us about three months ago, saying she had been kicked out of her home because she refused to have an abortion. We found her a spot at the group home, and she has been there ever since. She looked at your portfolio and is very interested in your family. There is one catch. She really is looking for an open adoption. She wants to be able to stay in limited contact with the baby over the years. Have you and Stan ever discussed that option?" Renea paused to let Kelly process the information.

Kelly's heart beat wildly in her chest. *Open adoption?* she thought. *I don't know about that*, doubt rising every second. Instead of voicing the growing doubt Kelly chose to say instead, "Renea, I will talk to Stan about this, but I am sure we will want to at least meet her."

Kelly arrived at Harvey's restaurant ten minutes late. The long drive from the country had won yet again. She hurried into the restaurant, too late to let nervousness overtake her.

She is probably nervous enough for the both of us, she thought, as the hostess led her to the table and her waiting dinner date.

Renea had arranged for the girl, Tessa Thomas, to meet Kelly and Stan in a neutral location. Harvey's restaurant seemed the perfect place. The lighting and seating arrangements encouraged long conversation, but there was enough activity to cover any awkward silences. At the last minute, Stan had been called out of town on business, but both agreed Kelly should keep the appointment. "It may be better this way," Stan had said. "She may feel more comfortable meeting you first."

And so it was that Kelly approached the table in the corner alone. She noticed the slim girl with long, chestnut hair and thought, *She doesn't even look pregnant*. That is, until she walked to her seat and saw her protruding belly, barely hidden under a black coat.

"Tessa? I'm Kelly. It's nice to meet you."

The beautiful young girl looked up at Kelly with shining hazel eyes. It took all she had to keep from staring. The most unusual sensation passed over her as she saw Tessa's face for the first time. It was as if she were looking in a mirror. The hair was slightly different in cut and color, and even sitting Kelly could tell she was much taller than the petite girl in front of her. But the eyes. Not just the color of her eyes, though they clearly matched Kelly's eye color. No, it was more than the color. It was the look of brokenness and resolve she related to so strongly. *She is me*, Kelly thought with surprise. *She is me, years ago.*

Kelly quickly hid her reaction and sat down to make small talk. It didn't take long for the two to relax, and Kelly was surprised with how open Tessa was with information about her life. What Kelly didn't know was that Tessa was just as surprised at her openness. There was something about Kelly that felt comfortable—safe even. And before they had finished their meal, Tessa had made her decision. She would select Kelly to be the mother of her child. And if Kelly accepted, Tessa knew her baby would instantly gain what she herself had always longed for—a loving and stable home.

As they finished the last bites of their meal, the waiter came to refill their glasses of Coca-Cola and set a dessert menu before them. Kelly saw Tessa eye the menu with interest as she shyly asked, "Do you want to share some dessert?"

At that moment, Kelly knew her time of fasting was over. She was certain she had found her son. "Sure! I love dessert!" she replied with a confident smile.

CHAPTER

34

As Kelly hung up the phone, the details discussed with Renea were fresh on her mind. New Beginnings would allow Tessa to live with Kelly and Stan throughout the rest of the pregnancy.

"Yes, this is unusual," Renea had said. "We don't get many requests like this one. But given the fact Tessa wants an open adoption, we feel this will be a good test-run to see if that will work for all of you. You realize she could change her mind, don't you? Until she signs the relinquishment papers, she is free to change her mind at any point, regardless of where she has lived the final weeks of her pregnancy."

"Yes, I realize all that. I really think this is going to work out. But if it doesn't, at least Tessa will have experienced a stable home for a few weeks." Kelly replied, though a tiny bit of fear threatened her mind and heart.

And with that, Tessa had moved her meager belongings up to the spacious under-used playroom. Knowing Tessa was not used to being in a home with young children, Kelly and Stan made the playroom into somewhat of an apartment for Tessa. She had a bed and an old sofa. She had her own television, and even a desk with Stan's old computer. It was more than she could have ever imagined.

Kelly leaned against the kitchen counter and reminisced over the turn of events of the past two weeks. After their dinner at Harvey's, Kelly reached out to Tessa on a daily basis. She no longer saw her as the birth mother of her unborn son, but saw her as a needy child, in need of love and care. The desire to show God's love to Tessa was so strong, it was almost a compulsion. She couldn't stop herself, even if the rest of the world thought she was foolish.

She remembered her first conversation with Stan about Tessa moving in. It had not gone very well.

"I want her to stay," Kelly had simply said.

"We will have her back over to visit soon," Stan had replied.

She had turned toward him and looked at him intently, her eyes locked on his. She had paused just a moment, silently begging him to hear—really hear—her. "I want her to stay, Stan."

"What do you mean? She can't stay. We told the director we would have her back to the home by nine."

Kelly had looked out the window and had seen Tessa pushing the twins side-by-side on the swing set. She had smiled, had even looked peaceful, caught up temporarily in the beautiful moment of an ordinary day in the life of an ordinary family.

"Stan, listen, please," Kelly had said, willing him to understand. "She is the mother of our son. I don't want her in some home. I want her at our home."

"I don't think that would be very wise," Stan had said.

"You can't be serious. That just isn't done. It's too complicated. There are too many details and emotions to consider. You need to think of her. Will that really be the best thing for her? I mean ... after. That could get really, really hard for all of us."

Kelly had replied with words she felt just as strongly now as she did then. "I don't know about all that, Stan. I know people don't do this. I know our friends and family would think we were being foolish. But I don't really care. I just care about her."

The final words she had said that night, the ones that had eventually made their mark on Stan's hesitant yet faithful heart were these words: "Stan, when I look at her, I see me. It is the strangest sensation I have ever had. It's like looking in a mirror, only the mirror is a reflection of another me in another life," she had said.

Her precious Stan had opened his heart and his home to Tessa, just as she had. And together they trusted God alone to handle the repercussions of that choice.

CHAPTER

35

"I don't know why I let it happen," Tessa said to Kelly. She surprised herself by sharing so openly. But there was something safe about Kelly and Stan. Tessa knew deep inside she could trust them with the ugly truth of her mixed up life—at least she thought she could.

"I did know better. I knew the risks, but at the time I just didn't care," she paused and looked up at Kelly sizing up whether it was safe to continue. One look of judgment and she was out of there—at least emotionally. She had seen those looks before, had endured their looks and their whispers. One look like that from Kelly and the door to her heart would be sealed shut forever. But she didn't see that look. In fact, she saw just the opposite. For the first time she could remember, she saw acceptance.

She wouldn't accept me if she knew everything, she thought bitterly, anger rising in her chest. Defiantly she determined to test Kelly and prove her to be just like the rest.

"It wasn't my first time, you know," she said bluntly.

Kelly didn't speak, but looked at Tessa with even more

compassion than before, willing her to speak.

"Nope. My first time was long ago, much longer than you can imagine," bitterness forming in the inflection of her words and the look of her eyes. And that is when Kelly knew. She knew because she recognized the bitterness, she had felt it herself.

"Tessa, I understand," Kelly said quietly.

"Ha! Yeah, I'm sure you do," she replied sarcastically.

"Tessa, look at me. I know I look like I have a perfect life. I know you don't believe me when I say I understand, but I do. When I was about six …" she paused not wanting the pain to resurface again, yet willing to endure it, if it could help Tessa with her own. She looked down at her hands for several seconds and then looked intently at Tessa's eyes.

She spoke slowly and clearly pausing between words, "Tessa, I understand."

They both just sat there, looking at each other, once again seeing a reflection of the other.

Tessa had been living with Stan and Kelly for a month and was just a couple of weeks away from her due date. She had spent her days with Kelly following along as she prepared the nursery, bought groceries, and went to a women's Bible Study at their church. Tessa felt self-conscious as she entered the meeting room for the Bible Study the first time. Her belly was huge, and there was no way she could mask her present condition. And yet, the ladies of the group surrounded her with acceptance and love. It was a far cry from her last experience with church, but Tessa still found herself guarded and suspicious, waiting for the other shoe to drop, the snide comments, the whispering stares. To her great surprise, that never happened.

The week before the due date, Tessa and Kelly walked into Bible Study just as Sally Stevens, the leader of the study, began. Tessa was glad when they finally found a seat toward the back, very conscious of her bulging belly.

Sally began the study by saying, "Today we are going to look at a story from the book of First Samuel, chapter one. There was a certain man from Ramathaim, a Zuphite from the hill country of Ephraim, whose name was Elkanah. He had two wives; one was called Hannah and the other Peninnah. Peninnah had children, but Hannah had none. Year after year this man went up from his town to worship and sacrifice to the LORD Almighty at Shiloh, where Eli and his sons were priests of the LORD. Whenever the day came for Elkanah to sacrifice, he would give portions of the meat to his wife Peninnah and to all her sons and daughters. But to Hannah he gave a double portion because he loved her, and the LORD had closed her womb."

Kelly smiled as she remembered her closed womb and her double portion. *Thank you, Jesus*, she prayed silently.

Sally continued, "Year after year he went to worship and sacrifice to God. Year after year...this was not just a short-term problem. This was something that haunted her. And it affected her relationship with God. Each year they went to worship and sacrifice. This was a huge part of their lives. This was their chance to be close to God. You see, this was before Jesus died. And sacrifices were still necessary for a relationship with God. So Elkanah would give his wives and children each a portion to sacrifice. Peninnah had children, so there were several portions on her side of the family score card. Elkanah loved Hannah, and felt sorry for her, so he gave her a double portion. But she still had less. She had less to offer to her God. In her mind, she was unacceptable to God, and because the system based the allotment of sacrifices according to the number of children, she probably felt that she could never measure up. Hannah could not heal or even accept her lot because there was a constant source of irritation, rubbing salt in her wound. And she could not escape it. The source of irritation came from her own household. And many tears were shed."

Am I a source of irritation to Kelly? Tessa thought to herself, and without realizing what she was doing, leaned to the other side of the chair, away from Kelly.

"Let me stop right now and tell you about tears," Sally continued. "In Revelation we learn that one day God Himself will wipe away every tear from our eyes. Psalm 56:8 tells us that He saves our tears in a bottle. Our tears are precious to the Lord. He sees and feels every one of them. And He has already done something about them. In Isaiah, as well as in 1 Peter, we learn that 'by His wounds we are healed'. He wants to heal whatever hurts you have. And He can, praise the Lord!"

Have you stored my tears, God? Tessa thought. *I don't cry much anymore. I have learned to control it. But all those nights, when no one would see me … did You see me, God?*

"In verse 8, we see that Elkanah, her husband, would say to her, 'Hannah, why are you weeping? Why don't you eat? Why are you downhearted? Don't I mean more to you than ten sons?' Now, Elkanah sounds like a sweet man, and we are told that he did love Hannah very much, but he just didn't get it. This did not have anything to do with him. This was about a longing that Elkanah couldn't fill. Not just because he wasn't a child, but because this was about her and God. Hannah felt abandoned by God. Hannah felt that this longing kept her away from God. And it broke her heart," Sally said.

I understand that longing, Kelly thought.

I understand what it feels like to be abandoned by God, Tessa thought.

"Our deepest needs can only be met by God," Sally said. "Let me repeat that. Our deepest needs can only be met by God. No one and nothing can fill us in our deepest parts. And it is really disappointing when we try to place other people or other things in that place of deepest need, because it never really meets the need. It might give us a temporary relief, but then we are back to where we started. Only a close relationship with Jesus can fill us up and meet our deepest needs."

My deepest needs cannot be met by this baby, Kelly thought. *I know that is true. Don't let me forget, Lord.*

My deepest needs can't be met by having a real family? Tessa thought. *It sure would help, though.*

"Hannah began to make promises to the Lord," Sally continued. "In bitterness of soul Hannah wept much and prayed to the Lord. Have you ever wept 'in bitterness of soul'? I have. And she made a vow saying, 'O Lord Almighty, if you will only look upon your servant's misery and remember me, and not forget your servant…' Do you see the main problem? She felt like God had forgotten her. Have you ever felt that way? I have. But then the Holy Spirit will whisper truth once again to me. God tells us in Isaiah, *'Can a mother forget the baby at her breast and have no compassion on the child she has borne? Though she may forget I will not forget you! See, I have engraved you on the palms of my hands.'* Hannah was most afraid that the Lord had forgotten her. She promised that if He gave her a son, she would turn around and give him right back. She was vowing that she would devote her son to be a Nazirite. A Nazirite was a person who was especially devoted and consecrated and set apart for God's purposes. A person could become a Nazirite in two ways: first, if the individual made a vow to become a Nazirite for a specified amount of time; and secondly, as a lifelong devotion following a vow made on their behalf by a parent before their birth.

Lord, if You give me this son, I will give him back to you. He is Yours, Lord, Kelly prayed.

I could never forget my baby, Lord. I want what is best for him. And if Kelly and Stan are what is best, I will give him up. I will give him to You and to them, Tessa prayed.

"So in the course of time Hannah conceived and gave birth to a son. I think there is a lot of meaning in the phrase, 'in the course of time'," Sally said. "We don't know how long she still had to wait, but her waiting was different now. She waited in peace. Her surrender to God was real, and her life reflected the change. 'In the course of time'—not immediately, still time and probably more pain to go before the fruition of the plan, but her surrender and vow set the plan in motion. If she had her answer earlier, she would not have been to the point where she could totally surrender herself and her son to the Lord, and all of history would have been different. God had an enormous, extraordinary plan for Hannah and the world through Hannah that was much larger than she could have imagined. And it really was worth waiting for."

I know Your plans are good, Lord. I trust You, Kelly prayed.

Do you really have good plans for me, God? Even me? Tessa prayed.

"Hannah gave birth to a son, and named him Samuel, which means 'God has heard'," Sally said.

Kelly bowed her head and closed her eyes, thinking of her first born son, the one she named Samuel. *The one who would be just about Tessa's age, if he had lived,* she thought. She lifted her head and looked over at Tessa. A strange sensation passed over her at that moment, and words she had lived and savored before came to the forefront of her mind. *A double portion.*

Tessa looked at Kelly with a questioning glance, wondering what Kelly was thinking. But Kelly just smiled, then looked ahead at Sally.

"That is really what Hannah needed to know—that God heard her heart's cry," Sally continued. "He did hear, and He does hear ours. One of the first questions that comes to our minds, but sometimes we are afraid to ask is 'Why did God let the longing go on for so long?' Today, if you learn anything I hope it is that you do not have to be afraid of your feelings. God created the emotions inside of you. He is God. He can handle anything that you feel. You do not have to hide that from Him, for He knows it already. The quicker we acknowledge to Him how we really feel, or acknowledge the questions that we really have, the quicker He can transform our hearts with the renewing of our minds. Take everything to the Lord in prayer. When you pray, God always answers you. Sometimes He answers yes. Sometimes He answers no. Sometimes He answers wait."

"God sometimes answers no. Sometimes the no is because it is something that is not right or good for us. God sometimes answers no because we live in a fallen world that will not be made right until the end of time."

Kelly thought of her mom, laying day after day at Traceway Manor. *Yep, God sometimes answers no,* she thought.

"God sometimes answers wait," Sally continued. "God sometimes answers wait, because the details are not in place yet. God sometimes answers wait, because the glory will be even greater when the answer comes. If God answers no or wait, we can rest assured that His ways are higher than what we can see right now."

Once again Kelly felt a strange sensation and glanced over at Tessa.

"Hannah trusted God and all of His answers. She kept her promise and brought her son to Eli the priest and she said to him, 'As surely as you live, my lord, I am the woman who stood here beside you praying to the LORD. I prayed for this child, and the LORD has granted me what I asked of him. So now I give him to the LORD. For his whole life he will be given over to the LORD.' I imagine Hannah, gathering her courage, silently whispering a prayer for strength, and taking her young boy's hand, her precious answer to prayer, and saying, 'Remember me, Eli? I was the one who was in such despair. Well, here is my answer to all those prayers. And I am giving him back to God, and to you, too, Eli. For his whole life, I won't take him back."

Will Tessa give up her son? To God and to me? Kelly thought. *Can I give him up?* Tessa thought.

"When Hannah delivered her precious young son to live in the temple with Eli, she was not filled with the sorrow that we would expect. Instead, she prayed a victorious, joyful prayer.

She prayed, 'My heart rejoices in the LORD; in the LORD my horn is lifted high. My mouth boasts over my enemies, for I delight in your deliverance There is no one holy like the LORD; there is no one besides you; there is no Rock like our God.' In the midst of surrendering her son, Hannah's heart was filled with praise and thankfulness."

Lord, I surrender to Your will and Your plans, Kelly prayed.

Lord, give me the strength to surrender, Tessa prayed.

With those final prayers, they looked at each other and smiled.

CHAPTER

36

Two days later, Kelly heard a knock at her bedroom door just after midnight. She quickly rose to open the door and there found Tessa bent over in pain.

"Is it time?" Kelly asked anxiously.

"I don't know for sure. It could be Braxton Hicks—those pre-contractions the doctor warned me about. But it hurts, and it comes pretty regularly. Do you think it's time?"

"I'm not sure," Kelly replied honestly. She was well aware this was like the blind leading the blind. "I've never had a baby, but it sounds like what I've seen on TV. Why don't I call the doctor?"

"Thanks. I think I would feel better if you did." Tessa replied, as she winced through another pinching pain.

The doctor suggested they come in to be checked and an hour later he confirmed she was in active labor. Kelly and Stan quickly began to make all the calls to family and friends, knowing the late hour did not matter. They called Will and Kelly's sisters. Then they called Stan's parents and his sister, Catherine. All were filled with joy at the news, all promised to pray. As Stan hung up the last phone call, Kelly looked over at Tessa propped up in the hospital bed, already dressed in the hospital gown. Tessa was crying. It was the first time Kelly had ever seen her cry, despite the fact that they had been together for weeks now.

"Tessa, what's wrong? Are you hurting?" Kelly asked with concern.

Tessa simply shook her head as tears continued to stream down her cheeks.

"Are you scared? I know I would be scared."

Tessa shook her head once again, and tried in vain to wipe away the steady stream of tears.

"What's wrong, Honey? You can talk to me," Kelly replied.

"It's just … I don't have anyone to call. I can't think of a single person who would want me to wake them up in the middle of the night to celebrate the birth of this baby. I just don't have anyone," she said as she closed her eyes trying to stop the flow.

Kelly took Tessa's hands in hers and said, "Tessa, look at me."

Tessa obediently opened her eyes and looked into Kelly's sincere face as she said, "You have us. Don't forget that. We are here with you and for you. Okay?"

Tessa simply nodded, took a deep breath, and braced herself for the next contraction.

CHAPTER

37

A week later, Kelly walked up the steps of the church, and headed toward the meeting room for Bible Study. She had baby Jack gently tucked inside a papoose, close to her heart. She loved to feel his tiny warmth against her chest and hear his newborn grunts and stirring. It had been a roller coaster week, that's for sure. As she walked down the hallway, she reflected on the past week.

Jack was born in the wee hours of the morning on October 10, 2009. His first cries were mingled with the laughter and joyful tears of both Kelly and Stan. Tessa's own tears flowed, but at the time, Kelly couldn't gauge what kind of tears they were.

Keeping with their open adoption plan, Kelly and Stan brought Tessa back home with them to recuperate until she could return home to her grandmother. They estimated she would stay for about eight weeks, until the end of the school semester. Her recovery had been rough so far. She had returned to the hospital with an excruciating headache from a spinal fluid leak caused by the epidural. Once she returned home with Kelly and Stan, she spent her time as instructed laying lifeless on the couch. She didn't want to do anything but lay very still—and hold Jack. Kelly obliged her request over and over, and each time a cautious feeling signaled warning in her heart.

She is too attached to him, Kelly worried.
She wants to hold him all the time, she fretted.
She is going to change her mind, she concluded.

And the gentle whisper of her Good Shepherd said, "He is not your child, Kelly. He is not even Tessa's child. He is My child. Surrender him to Me." And so she did, as heart-wrenching as it was. Over and over, she surrendered Jack to the Lord and continued to love Tessa with the same unconditional love she herself had experienced.

When Tessa had to return to the hospital a second time for a blood patch so the headaches would cease, they decide to let her recuperate at Stan's parents' home. She needed more rest than a house full of toddler twins and a newborn could offer. Not to mention the nervousness they all felt with the looming decision yet to be made.

When Kelly left for Bible Study, she stopped to see Tessa, just had she had each day. Renea had arrived at Stan's parents' house with the relinquishment papers. Kelly did not know whether Tessa would sign them or not. She seemed so torn. And so sad. All of the warnings Kelly had heard from well-meaning family and friends, came back to haunt her. Renea left the papers and promised to return in the afternoon.

Kelly laid on the bed beside Tessa, and put Jack between them. "When can I come home?" Tessa asked.

"As soon as you feel up to it," Kelly replied honestly. "But we need to talk about the situation before us. Tessa, you don't have to sign the papers. You don't have to give us Jack. It is still your choice. And I want you to know we will love you even if you change your mind. Even if you change your mind, you can continue to live with us until the end of the semester. Above all, I want you to know that God loves you and we love you—no strings attached. But if you decide to sign the papers, you have to give us the chance to bond with Jack. You have to let us do what you selected us to do—be his parents. He has to bond with me and then with Stan. He has to bond with the twins. And then, I would be happy for him to bond with you, as well. Because I am certain you will always be an important part of his life—and an important part of all of our lives. You already are."

Tessa simply nodded, and Kelly scooped up Jack and headed off to Bible Study, anxious to hear truth from God's Word to sustain her no matter what the coming days revealed.

God, did I hear You wrong? Kelly prayed as she reached out to open the door to the meeting room. *Did I just want what I wanted, not what You wanted? I surrender to You and Your will once again.*

After Kelly returned to see Tessa, she was surprised to find her sitting on the couch, dressed and ready to go home. Kelly sat on the couch beside her, and took hold of her hand.

"I signed the papers," Tessa said.

"Are you sure?" Kelly said.

"I am positive," Tessa replied. "There was never any real doubt in my mind, Kelly. I know this is what is best for him—and for me."

"Tessa, I can't imagine how hard this is for you. I couldn't do it. I *didn't* do it. We would totally understand if you changed your mind.

"I won't. It never was really about not wanting to sign the

papers. It wasn't so much about not wanting to give up Jack. It was about the fact that I didn't want to give up all of you. I just want a family, Kelly. A real family who won't leave. Who will love me even when I mess up. I just want all of you," Tessa said, as a lone tear streamed down her cheek.

"Well, come on then," Kelly replied. "Let's go home."

Eight weeks turned into eight months; then a year passed and two more after that, and still Tessa stayed. It would have broken Stan and Kelly's heart if she had decided to leave, though they would never have told her that. They wanted her to be free to do exactly what was best for her. And so far, that best had been to bond into a family of six.

One day in March, 2013, Tessa got a call from her grandmother saying she was sick and in the hospital. Tessa had kept in touch with Grandma, calling her weekly and sending her photos of Jack and her new family. Kelly offered to drive her to the hospital, but Tessa wanted to go alone. When she arrived, Grandma was alone and sleeping. She actually looked peaceful and happy, the rough corners of her personality seemed to have changed—*or maybe I am the one who has changed*, Tessa thought.

"Hey, Grandma," Tessa gently said, unsure of whether she should wake her or not.

Grandma's eyes fluttered open, and she blinked several times to clear the fog. "Tessa, is that you, child?"

"Yes, ma'am. It's me." Tessa replied.

Grandma's bottom lip quivered just a bit, which was a strange sight for Tessa to see. She had never seen Grandma express much emotion—except irritation.

"Tessa, I'm glad you came. I wanted the chance to tell you something." She paused a moment and struggled to sit up in bed. Tessa rushed to her side and helped her sit up, just as she had so many times before.

When she was settled, she looked Tessa in the eyes and cleared her throat. "I wanted to tell you this: You did the right thing, Tessa. The brave thing. I'm glad you had Jack. I'm glad you have Kelly and Stan and the whole family. You deserve that, Tessa. You are a good girl. You deserve to be happy. I'm sorry for the times I made life harder for you. But I hope you know I always loved you," she said, as emotion caused her voice to crack in a most unnatural way.

"I know that, Grandma. I love you, too." Tessa replied.

And in typical Grandma fashion the moment was over and the gruff irritation returned. "Okay then, girl. Go get me something to eat."

Tessa smiled and kissed her cheek and headed to the cafeteria to find something to please her grandmother.

A month later, Tessa received another phone call. This one told her of her grandmother's passing. Tessa cried when she heard the news. And Kelly held her and prayed over her. And as Kelly held her, the tears of grief mixed with tears of relief, for Tessa knew for sure she was not alone.

CHAPTER

Kelly, Stan, and Tessa drove to Wesley United Methodist Church and parked in a spot near the entrance. Only a few cars were scattered in the spacious parking lot of the church. Stan prayed over Tessa before getting out of the car.

"Lord, I ask that You would give Tessa strength to say goodbye. I pray she would have no root of bitterness, and that the only memories she savors would be the happy ones. I pray that You would give her strength to face whomever she needs to face this day." Kelly and Tessa joined their voices with Stan's voice in a sincere "Amen". There was no need to point out the obvious. Tessa, Kelly, and Stan all knew it was very possible that Tessa would face her mother this day. It had been years since she had last seen her. And the nervousness of that meeting was as strong as the emotion of laying her grandmother to rest.

They waited in the car until five minutes before the appointed time, then walked in together. Kelly and Stan encouraged Tessa to go sit with the family, and they took a seat toward the back. They wanted to be there for Tessa, and they also wanted to be sensitive to the situation.

The service was simple and direct, just as Grandma would have wanted. Tessa chose to ride with Kelly and Stan in the processional to the cemetery. A few final words were spoken, a final prayer was prayed, and then those in attendance began to slowly make their way back to the cars.

As they walked to their car, Tessa stopped suddenly in her tracks. Standing a few feet ahead of her was her mom. *She looks so different without Roy and Silvia by her side*, Tessa thought. Kelly encouraged Tessa to go talk to her and Tessa obliged. Kelly and Stan watched Tessa and Tammy talking earnestly and in a few minutes they hugged each other tightly. They walked hand in hand toward Kelly and Stan. Tammy looked weary and fragile, but perfectly serene when she reached out to wrap Kelly in a sincere embrace. When they parted, Tammy looked into Kelly's eyes, with tears falling from her own, and said, "Thank you. Thank you for taking such good care of Tessa. I am forever indebted to you."

Tears filled Kelly's eyes as she reached out for another hug. "It is my great pleasure," she replied.

Peace and relief flooded Tessa's heart as she watched both of her mothers embrace each other—the mother of her past, and the mother of her future. "Thank you, Lord," she whispered.

In December of that year Kelly met Tessa for lunch at a downtown café. It was one of their favorite spots—complete with old-time diner tables and chairs, original artwork, and most importantly, the most delicious peanut butter pie.

As they ate, they talked of Tessa's classes at the local college and the latest sales at the mall. They engaged in all of the normal day to day conversation of close family members. After their meal, however, Kelly noticed Tessa grew silent and began to pick at her pie rather than devour it.

In the keen sense of a mother, Kelly asked, "Tessa is something on your mind?"

"Not really," Tessa replied unconvincingly.

"Are you sure? You know I will listen," Kelly replied.

"Well, it's just that I have been thinking. About God. About all that He has done for me." She looked at Kelly who simply nodded for her to continue.

"Kelly, I never could have imagined all this. I didn't deserve it. But He gave it all to me anyway. You, Stan, Jack, the twins—my own room," she looked at Kelly with a twinkle in her eye.

She looked down at her pie to gather her thoughts, and then continued. "I want to tell the world that I belong to Him, Kelly. He has done far more than I could have ever hoped or imagined. I want to give Him my heart and my whole life."

Kelly smiled a knowing smile. "Tessa, God has just answered my prayers once again!"

Two weeks later Tessa stood before their church congregation in the celebration of baptism. As she climbed down into the cool water, she knew this was another new beginning. As she rose up from the water, in the name of the Father, the Son, and the Holy Spirit, she knew this was the best new beginning she would ever experience.

A year later, Tessa stood before the congregation once

again. Bryan, the family's pastor and good friend, greeted the congregation during the time of offering.

"This is our time in the service where we celebrate with those offering their lives," he began, "But this one is a bit unusual. Come on Stan and Kelly, with your family," he said as he motioned them to join him on stage.

"Earlier this year, we celebrated with Tessa as she offered her life to Christ in baptism. Baptism is a great sign of our recognition of God claiming us. But today Tessa joins the Williams family. She's been a part of their world, a part of their lives; but today we rejoice as she becomes legally and officially theirs. I want to begin this time with watching this video."

Kelly and Stan had put together a video of family photos taken during the years Tessa had been a part of the family. Photos of Tessa with Stan and Kelly, Tessa with the twins, Tessa and Jack. Family trips, fun events, holidays, silly moments. Family photos. Her family. As soon as the video began, the voice-over on the video began. It was the voice of her new parents. Back and forth, Kelly and Stan took turns reading a letter they had written to Tessa. The words read pierced her heart, and tears formed in the corners of her eyes.

Dear Tessa,

Many years ago we began our journey with infertility. As we struggled, we asked God to take away the desire to become parents if it was not in His plans for us, but the desire only grew stronger.

We knew you were special from the moment we met you. You are strong and courageous. You persevere in spite of all you have had to endure. Instead of becoming bitter and angry, you choose to push forward. You are an inspiration. You have given so much!

You are a blessing and as time passes it becomes more and more clear that you are meant to be our child! We promise as your parents, we will not be perfect. We will make mistakes and probably let you down, but we also promise to love unconditionally and be your family forever.

Keep your heart open. Remember, sometimes when God answers 'no' it is a gift. If He had given us what we thought we wanted all those years ago, we would have missed out on you and Jack and Bella and Evie.

You are a holy heir! Sent to us from a Father who has always loved you and has always been with you. We are only a symbol of what His great love is and will be in your life.

God created you with a purpose. He is already using you in a mighty way. If you will allow Him, He will complete His good work that He started in you. It is an honor to be your parents!

We love you so much!
Mom and Dad

He settles the barren woman in her home as a happy mother of children.

Psalm 114:9

As the video ended, Tessa wiped her eyes as Bryan roughly brushed at his own, and his voice cracked with emotion as he said, "Just as we celebrated Tessa's adoption into the family of God through baptism, we now celebrate Tessa's adoption into the Williams family. God sets the precedent for this. Adoption was God's idea. When we had done everything to separate ourselves from Him—to be outside of His family, outside His family tree—He went to extraordinary links to graft us in. Ephesians 1:3-5 says *'All praise to God, the Father of our Lord Jesus Christ, who has blessed us with every spiritual blessing in the heavenly realms because we are united with Christ. Even before he made the world, God loved us and chose us in Christ to be holy and without fault in his eyes. God decided in advance to adopt us into his own family by bringing us to himself through Jesus Christ. This is what he wanted to do, and it gave him great pleasure.'"*

As Bryan spoke, Kelly stood with one arm wrapped around Tessa, the other hand resting on the head of their shared son. The twins stood closely behind their big sister, with Stan standing nearby as a watchman over all of them.

"Today we celebrate with Stan and Kelly, Bella, Evie, Jack, and Tessa that Stan and Kelly have adopted Tessa into their own family. This has brought them great joy, and we share in that joy. Would you help me welcome Tessa *Williams* to our church family?"

The congregation rose to their feet with applause, as many of them had walked the long journey with this precious family.

"Now, will you extend a hand toward Tessa and the whole Williams family and join me as we pray over them? Lord, we thank You for this marvelous expression of Your grace and love for us. That You brought us into your family, not because of who we were but because of who You are. And having been so loved, You give us the capacity to love. Lord, I celebrate this capacity in Stan and Kelly and in Tessa and I pray that love that has begun and flourished would come to full bloom, that all the ways and intimacy of family would be known and that Tessa would not only rejoice in this moment but that she may walk in these truths and in the fullness of this love all the days of her life. We rejoice with Stan and Kelly and their family and we pray that You would bless them in the days ahead. In the powerful name of Jesus, Amen."

With the final amen, the congregation erupted in applause once more.

CHAPTER

39

On the second Wednesday in October, 2015, Kelly received a call from her dad. "Hey, Honey," he began when she answered her cell phone. "Have you seen your mom this week?"

"Yes, I went to visit on Monday. Why? Is something wrong?"

"No. Well, I don't think so. I don't know. I just left there. Something seemed different today. I just wondered if you had noticed anything."

"Everything seemed the same to me. She still has that terrible sore which won't heal. That is bound to hurt. What did you notice?"

"Well, I know this sounds silly. It's probably nothing. But when I visited at lunchtime, she just kept looking up in the corner. It was as if she was seeing something. She kept straining to look in the corner the whole time I was there. Then she would look at me, as if she wanted me to see something, too. I know that sounds weird."

"Do you want me to go out there this afternoon?"

"I hate to ask you to do that, but yeah, I think that would be a good idea."

A couple of hours later, Kelly stood before the heavy gray door, once again pausing in prayer before she entered the room. Just as Will had said, Sadie's gaze was on a spot up in the corner of the room. "Hey, Mom," Kelly said.

Sadie slowly moved her eyes toward Kelly and blinked several times. She had lost all communication, but she still could move her eyes and occasionally her head. After a few seconds, her gaze returned to the invisible scene which had captured her attention.

Kelly walked toward the bed and sat down in the nearest chair. She scooted the chair closer to her mother and took her hand. Still Sadie continued her gaze toward the corner of the room. As Kelly took her mother's hand, she noticed it felt very warm. She then placed her hand on Sadie's forehead and grimaced. She was definitely running a fever. Kelly left the room to tell the nurse and call her dad.

"Dad, I am at Traceway. Mom is running a fever. And you are right, she is acting differently. She keeps looking up at the corner. I know you are working until 5:30, but you may want to take off a little early tonight."

"I'll be right there," he replied.

By the next morning, Sadie was running a fever of 105. Ice packs and cold compresses were applied, and medicine was increased, but by mid-morning they were calling in the family. The time had come and they all knew it. By late afternoon, the family had gathered together in her mother's room. Will, Kelly, Addi, and Molly surrounded Sadie, each telling her it was okay to leave. Even still, labored breath after labored breath, Sadie struggled to hold on to life, just as she always had done. She had long outlived her prognosis, despite the deplorable things she had to endure.

As night turned to early morning, one by one, everyone left to get to some sleep--even Will, after Kelly insisted and hospice reassured him that her vital signs were stable. But Kelly couldn't seem to take her own advice and lingered on throughout the night.

About two a.m., Kelly crawled in bed with her mom, just as she had throughout her childhood. She opened her Bible to Psalm 23 and read it aloud over and over.

The Lord is my shepherd;
I shall not want.
He makes me to lie down in green pastures;
He leads me beside the still waters.
He restores my soul;
He leads me in the paths of righteousness
For His name's sake.
Yea, though I walk through the valley
of the shadow of death,
I will fear no evil;
For You are with me;
Your rod and Your staff, they comfort me.
You prepare a table before me in the presence of my enemies;
You anoint my head with oil;
My cup runs over.
Surely goodness and mercy shall follow me
All the days of my life; And I will dwell
in the house of the Lord forever.

Oh, how Kelly hated to hear the sound of her mother's labored breathing. It was as if she were gasping for air while the MS-ravaged muscles choked her with heart-wrenching force. Finally, with tears streaming down her face, Kelly took both of her mother's hands and looked into her brilliant blue eyes.

"Mama, you have to let go," she cried. "You have been the best mama; you have been the best wife. We all love you so much. But it is okay to let go. We will be okay. We will take care of Daddy. I promise. You have grandchildren in heaven you have never seen. And your parents. You will get to see them again, Mama. And one day we will all be there together. It's okay to let go." Her mother then strained her neck turning her gaze once again to the invisible scene in the corner of the room.

"Is it an angel, Mama? Or is it Jesus Himself? Go with Him, Mom."

Kelly then got up and kneeled beside the bed, weeping. "Lord, I don't know what to do to help her get home to You. Help her, Lord. Heal her once and for all."

Moments later, her labored breathing quieted. Her eyes remained fixed on the corner of the room, but instead of the struggle she had exhibited before, there was peace. The hospice nurse came in to check her vital signs. They were now dropping. It was time to call Will and her sisters. Within minutes, the original family of five were once again surrounding Sadie's bed. By 6 a.m. her eyes were closed and each breath grew farther and farther apart. An hour later, the nurses asked them all to leave the room so they could examine her more closely.

Just as Will and Kelly re-entered the room, Sadie took

her last breath. They all stood in stunned silence for a few moments, unable to believe she was really gone. As if on cue, they all felt the wound of great loss, and guttural, unnatural sobbing overtook them all. After several minutes of being lost in the raging sea of grief, Will sat up and took a deep breath.

He said loud enough to be heard over the sounds of breaking hearts, "Can you imagine what she is experiencing right now?"

With those words, peace entered that room of grief and the hope of heaven descended upon all of them. If they could have seen across the veil which separates heaven and earth, they would have seen Sadie, shining with love and joy. Sadie, standing with strength and dignity. Sadie, holding the hand of a boy named Samuel with adorable twins running joyfully near by. And behind her, every child Kelly and Stan lost were playing happily with generations of family and friends gathered together. There was peace and love and wholeness. And Sadie smiled, knowing she was finally free of the body which had held her captive for so long.

CHAPTER

Tessa sat beside the tub and poured a cup of warm water over Jack's head. Kelly had showed her how to make him close his eyes, and lift his head so the shampoo would not sting his eyes. "Eyes closed, head toward heaven," she repeated several times in a sing-song fashion, just as she had heard Kelly say on numerous occasions. That was one of her favorite parts of being in a family. Tessa watched and learned so many things—things she would never have learned if she had not come to be a part of this home, this family. Not just little things like how to wash a toddler's hair; but big things like how to pray, how to fight fair, how to choose each other every day. She was beyond grateful.

Tessa turned to grab the clean towel she had placed on the counter, then helped Jack stand up in the water while she wrapped the warm towel around him. She lifted him up and gave him a big hug, as water dripped down his little legs and toes, wetting her shirt and the floor beneath them. Suddenly a terrible snap and crash echoed through the bathroom, causing both to jump forcefully. Tessa instinctively held tightly to Jack, determined to protect him from the unknown source of the terrible sound. She quickly looked toward the tub and saw the bare space on the wall where the heavy antique mirror had just hung. It lay awkwardly in the bathtub, in the exact spot where Jack had sat only moments before. The realization of the tragedy which could have been reality caused Tessa to go weak in the knees. Still holding tightly to Jack, Tessa sat on the wet floor, too stunned to do anything else.

Kelly came running at the sound, and the sight of Tessa in the floor with Jack sent cold dread through her veins. "Tessa! Are you okay? Is Jack okay? What happened?" she asked in rapid succession.

Tessa, still shaken, took a deep breath and said, "We are both okay. The mirror fell from the wall. Kelly, I had just gotten Jack out of the tub. It could have hurt him," she said in a shaky voice. She buried her face in the towel and cried.

Kelly joined them on the wet floor and wrapped her arms around her daughter and her son. "But it didn't, praise God," she said, in a trembling voice. Her arms and legs began to shake with the "What-Ifs" which flooded her mind. They sat in silence wrapped in the warmth of each other until the uncomfortable moisture served as a motivation to move off the floor. Still trembling both struggled to rise.

"I should have hung that mirror with a screw instead of a nail," she said as she handed Tessa another towel. Jack scrambled out of Tessa's arms and ran naked through the bedroom anxious to tell Bella and Evie all about the incident. Kelly and Tessa wiped the water off the floor then together worked to lift the heavy mirror out of the bathtub. Still in its frame, the mirror was cracked in four irregular quadrants with squiggly lines of broken mirror within each quadrant. They leaned it up against the sink and stepped back to see their distorted reflections in the broken mirror.

A thoughtful look covered Kelly's features as if she suddenly had a great revelation which brought peace and calm to her emotions. "Tessa, I want to tell you something. This mirror was my grandmother's mirror. It has endured for a long time. I remember it hanging in her house when I was a little girl, and my mom gave it to me when she died. I remember one day when I was a little girl my grandmother tried to teach me a verse from the Bible, 1 Corinthians 13:12. She helped me memorize it as we stood by this mirror and had me look in the mirror as I repeated it after her over and over. Now, my grandmother only believed in King James version of the Bible. *It has been good enough for Christians for three hundred years, so it should be good enough for you,* she always said, although when the New King James version came out, she relented. So she had me memorize it in the New King James version. It went like this: *For now we see in a mirror, dimly, but then face to face. Now I know in part, but then I shall know just as I also am known.*

The truth is, I never really understood that verse. But recently, I found it in another translation, the New Life Version. It said the same thing, only differently—in a way I understood it better. It said: *Now that which we see is as if we were looking in a broken mirror. But then we will see everything. Now I know only a part. But then I will know everything in a perfect way. That is how God knows me right now.*

You see, Tessa, life is like this broken mirror. We can still see in it. We can make out our reflection. But it is not quite clear at the points of brokenness. That is how life on this earth is, and probably always will be until we get to heaven. We can see parts of it clearly, other parts not so much. But we just need to hang on, trusting God, until He reveals all the intricate parts of His good plan. He will weave all the good and all the bad together in such a beautiful and perfect way. Now we know in part—just in fragments. But then we will know fully all the ways He has saved us and helped us and redeemed us—even when we couldn't see He was working. In heaven, we will finally know our whole story, just as we have been fully known by God, even now. Does that make any sense at all?" Kelly asked with a smile.

"Yeah, I think so," Tessa replied. And even if she didn't fully understand all Kelly had said, she knew she would one day—and for now that was enough.

The End

In Loving Memory of
Sara Humphrey Biddle
September 12, 1949—October 9, 2015

*...To have and to hold
from this day forward,
for better, for worse,
for richer, for poorer,
in sickness and in health,
to love and to cherish,
until we are parted by death.
This is my solemn vow.*

A Word From
Kelly Williams

This book is loosely based on my life. Although names and circumstances surrounding events have been changed, the message of God's unconditional love and power to heal all wounds is the ultimate unshakable truth. There are no words to describe how God took a life that I thought was too damaged and dirty and changed it into a masterpiece. No drug, person, or experience I could ever dream up is anything compared to the fullness I have lived since turning my life over to Jesus. Let me be clear, this does not mean there are no more trials, but in these trials there is hope and a "peace that passes all understanding".

Dear friend, I do not know where you have been but I know that God created you with a purpose—with plans to prosper and not harm you. Please don't wait another second to ask Him to be your Savior and watch with great expectation as God does immeasurably more than you could ask or imagine!

May God pour out His richest blessings upon you!
Kelly

PS What a gift my husband, Stan, is to me and our children. I am grateful to God for his unconditional acceptance, love, and support.

To schedule a speaking engagemen email Kelly at kellywilliamsministries@gmail.com
www.kellywilliamsministries.com

A Word From
Sara W. Berry

A Broken Mirror is a novel. However, the core of the story is true. In fact, only God could have written such a detailed, amazing story. I am simply a storyteller. I pray I have been a faithful steward. All the glory goes to Him alone.

Names, settings, dates, and details have been changed to protect the privacy of those included in the story. In parts, one character in the story may represent a group of people in real life. Many parts came from my imagination. But, as is often the case, truth is better than fiction, and with that in mind, I have kept many of the details of the story as they were experienced.

The details of what happened in this story are not as important as the beautiful redemption the characters experienced. I want you to know that God is writing your story, too. Let Him have His way in your life, and you will find an intricate, fulfilling plot, written just for you.

Kelly and I would love to hear from you and pray for you. Let us know your own story. We know it will be a masterpiece.

Trusting in the One who loves us best,
Sara
www.sarawberry.com

To schedule a speaking engagement, email Sara at info@bethelroadpublications.com

About
Sara W. Berry

Sara W. Berry, author and creator of many Bethel Road products, has been teaching, be it in a classroom setting or church setting, for the past 17 years. Her experience began at Millsaps College in Jackson, Mississippi where she received a Bachelor of Science Degree in Education, as well as numerous education and leadership awards.

Her varied work experience includes teaching elementary students in Memphis, TN; Nashville, TN; Jackson, MS; Costa Rica and Ecuador. She was director of a tutorial program for inner city children in Stanson, MS as well as program director for an inner city humanitarian service in Memphis, TN. She also served as children's director for her church.

Her teaching experience continues each day as she is rearing her seven children: Katie, Ellie, Joseph, Troy Joshua, Sally, and Charlie. She is married to Dr. Mont Berry. Without his loving support, she could not fulfill God's calling on her life.

Sara has an intense love for discipleship. She desires to teach through her books and curriculum, the truth of God's Word, knowing that the Word does not return void. Sara has an equal passion for missions. She has taken seriously the mandate of the Great Commission. She lived in San Jose, Costa Rica as a missionary teacher in the late 1980s. After her marriage to Mont, they both lived in Shell Mera, Ecuador, he working at a jungle hospital, she teaching at the Nate Saint Memorial School. Most recently, the entire Berry family spent time in mission service in Peru and Nicaragua. In recent years, Sara also spent time in China, where she has ministered as well as adopted her two youngest children. Several of Sara's programs have been translated into Spanish, Chinese.

With the gift of teaching, and a passion for discipleship, Sara finds great joy in sharing the truth of the Scriptures with others. Sara has shared with thousands of women from the United States, South America, and China. If you are interested in scheduling a speaking engagement, or for information on any other books or teaching materials by Sara W. Berry, email us at info@bethelroadpublications.com.

More books by Sara W. Berry include:
A Cord of Three Strands, (with Tricia J. Robbins)
Beyond Bethel book and workbook
Stones from the River Jordan book and workbook

For Children:
The Integrity Time Series
The Pirate, the Princess, and the Precious Treasure
A Home for Him

www.bethelroadpublications.com

Book Club Questions

Why do you think the author selected the title, *A Broken Mirror*?

How was Tessa a mirrored reflection of Kelly—in what ways were they similar?

In what ways were they different?

How was Kelly a mirrored reflection of Sadie—in what ways were they similar?

In what ways were they different?

How do you think Will displayed Christ-like characteristics?

Kelly believed God promised her a double portion. How was that double portion revealed in the story?

In Chapter 38, Bryan points out that adoption was God's idea. He said, "When we had done everything to separate ourselves from Him—to be outside of His family, outside of His family tree—He went to extraordinary lengths to graft us in." How did God graft us into His family through spiritual adoption?

Redemption is a theme throughout the book. Name ways that redemption was realized.

The following are the meaning behind the names of the characters in the book. How does the meaning of their names relate to their experience?

Will: determined protector, steadfast guardian

Sadie: form of Sara, princess, royal one

Tessa: fourth child; harvester, reaper, sower

Jack: God is gracious, God is giving, transformation

Bella: form of Arabella, answered prayer

Evie: full of life

Addi: form of Addison, fiery one

Molly: dearly beloved

Chris: follower of Christ

Hope: Christian virtue, expectation, to help someone

Diving Deeper

In Chapter 21, Kelly went to a Bible Study where Noah was studied. Let's dive a little deeper into that story.

It was said of Noah, "he walked with God." What does that mean to you?

What is a covenant?

What was the sign of the covenant that God made with Noah?

Has God kept His promise?

Describe the episode that caused Noah to curse Ham and his descendents.

Read the following verses aloud:

Hatred stirs up dissension, but love covers over all wrongs.
Proverbs 10:12

He who covers over an offense promotes love, but whoever repeats the matter separates close friends.
Proverbs 17:9

Above all, love each other deeply, because love covers over a multitude of sins.
1 Peter 4:8

What are the common words found in all of these verses?

What does the word "cover" mean in relation to "love"?

What is the difference between covering an offense in love and denying sin and truth?

In Chapter 35, Kelly and Tessa attend another Bible Study together where Hannah was studied. Let's dive a little deeper into that story.

We find a vivid display of longing in the story of Hannah. Name a time when you experienced extreme longing.

What emotions did this longing stir up within you?

How did you endure the waiting?

Read Psalm 40:1-3, Psalm 27:13-14, Isaiah 30:18. What provisions does God offer us while waiting on Him?

Read Psalm 130:5-6 and Titus 2:13. What can we do while we wait?

Jeremiah 33:3 says, "Call to me and I will answer you and show you great and mighty things which you know not."

God always answers. He sometimes answers yes. He sometimes answers no. He sometimes answers wait. But He always answers.

Why do you think He sometimes answers *no*?

Why do you think He sometimes answers *wait*?

How does listening to God help you deal with *no* or *wait*?

Describe someone with good listening skills.

How could you develop better listening skills with your Heavenly Father?

Read 1 Kings 19:9-13. What areas of your life seem like the earthquake or the wind or the fire, those things which distract us from the gentle whisper of the Lord?

If you could imagine the gentle whispers of the Lord towards you, what would they say?

Read the following scriptures aloud, understanding that these are just a sampling of the Lord's gentle whispers, found in His Word. Listen carefully to these words, and know that He speaks them to each of us, His children.

Isaiah 49:15-16, "Can a mother forget the baby at her breast and have no compassion on the child she has borne? Though she may forget, I will

not forget you! See, I have engraved you on the palms of my hands…"
Jeremiah 29:11-13, "For I know the plans that I have for you," declares the Lord, "plans to prosper you and not to harm you, plans to give you hope and a future. Then you will call upon me and come and pray to me, and I will listen to you. You will seek me and find me when you seek me with all your heart. I will be found by you," declares the Lord.

Isaiah 1:18-19, "Come now, let us reason together," says the Lord. "Though your sins are like scarlet, they shall be white as snow; though they are red as crimson, they shall be like wool. If you are willing and obedient, you will eat the best from the land."

Jeremiah 33:3, "Call to me and I will answer you and tell you great and unsearchable things you do not know."

Isaiah 43: 1-2, "Fear not, for I have redeemed you; I have summoned you by name; you are mine. When you pass through the waters, I will be with you; and when you pass through the rivers, they will not sweep over you. When you walk through the fire, you will not be burned; the flames will not set you ablaze. For I am the Lord, your God, the Holy One of Israel, your Savior…."

Isaiah 42:16, "I will lead the blind by ways they have not known, along unfamiliar paths I will guide them; I will turn the darkness into light before them and make the rough places smooth. These are the things I will do; I will not forsake them."

How do each of these verses make you feel?

More Books by Sara W. Berry

www.bethelroadpublications.com